STAR WARS™
DOCTOR APHRA

STAR WARS™
DOCTOR APHRA

SARAH KUHN

NEW YORK

2022 Del Rey Trade Paperback Edition

Copyright © 2021 by Lucasfilm Ltd. & ® or ™ where indicated.
All rights reserved.
Excerpt from *Star Wars: Dooku: Jedi Lost* by Cavan Scott copyright
© 2019 by Lucasfilm Ltd. & ® or ™ where indicated. All rights reserved.

Published in the United States by Del Rey, an imprint of
Random House, a division of Penguin Random House LLC, New York.

DEL REY is a registered trademark and the CIRCLE colophon is a
trademark of Penguin Random House LLC.

Portions of this work are based on the Marvel Comics
series *Darth Vader* by Kieron Gillen and Salvador Larroca
as well as material from the *Star Wars* series by Jason Aaron,
Mike Deodato, and Leinil Francis Yu.

Originally published as an audiobook in the United States
and in hardcover by Del Rey, an imprint of Random House,
a division of Penguin Random House LLC, in 2021.

LIBRARY OF CONGRESS CATALOGING-IN-PUBLICATION DATA
Names: Kuhn, Sarah (Author), author.
Title: Doctor Aphra / Sarah Kuhn.
Other titles: At head of title: Star Wars
Description: New York: Del Rey, [2021]
Identifiers: LCCN 2020046602 (print) | LCCN 2020046603 (ebook) |
ISBN 9780593157251 (hardcover; acid-free paper) | ISBN 9780593357453
(trade paperback) | ISBN 9780593357033 (ebook)
Subjects: LCSH: Star Wars fiction. | GSAFD: Science fiction.
Classification: LCC PS3611.U3937 D63 2021 (print) | LCC PS3611.U3937
(ebook) | DDC 813/.6—dc23
LC record available at https://lccn.loc.gov/2020046602
LC ebook record available at https://lccn.loc.gov/2020046603

Printed in the United States of America on acid-free paper

randomhousebooks.com

1st Printing

Book design by Elizabeth A. D. Eno

For Emily Woo Zeller—thank you for giving Aphra a voice

THE STAR WARS NOVELS TIMELINE

THE HIGH REPUBLIC

Light of the Jedi
The Rising Storm
Tempest Runner
The Fallen Star

Dooku: Jedi Lost
Master and Apprentice

I THE PHANTOM MENACE

II ATTACK OF THE CLONES

Thrawn Ascendancy: Chaos Rising
Thrawn Ascendancy: Greater Good
Thrawn Ascendancy: Lesser Evil
Dark Disciple: A Clone Wars Novel

III REVENGE OF THE SITH

Catalyst: A Rogue One Novel
Lords of the Sith
Tarkin

SOLO

Thrawn
A New Dawn: A Rebels Novel
Thrawn: Alliances
Thrawn: Treason

ROGUE ONE

IV A NEW HOPE

Battlefront II: Inferno Squad
Heir to the Jedi
Doctor Aphra
Battlefront: Twilight Company

V THE EMPIRE STRIKES BACK

VI RETURN OF THE JEDI

The Alphabet Squadron Trilogy
The Aftermath Trilogy
Last Shot

Bloodline
Phasma
Canto Bight

VII THE FORCE AWAKENS

VIII THE LAST JEDI

Resistance Reborn
Galaxy's Edge: Black Spire

IX THE RISE OF SKYWALKER

DRAMATIS PERSONAE

DOCTOR CHELLI LONA APHRA: Rogue archaeologist. Weapons and droid expert extraordinaire. Our intrepid heroine.

DARTH VADER: Infamous Sith Lord. Man of few words. Our intrepid heroine's terrifying boss.

TRIPLE-ZERO: Protocol droid. Favorite hobbies include translation, holo-chess, and draining organics of all their blood.

BEETEE: Blastomech droid. Has a flamethrower.

SANA STARROS: Smuggler. Unfortunate dreamboat. Working with the rebels for some godsforsaken reason.

BLACK KRRSANTAN: Disgraced Wookiee. Fearsome bounty hunter. Do not challenge him to a pit fight.

PADMÉ AMIDALA: The "good" former queen and senator of Naboo.

PRINCESS LEIA ORGANA: Rebel royalty. Has a mean left hook.

LUKE SKYWALKER: Yellow-haired rebel humanoid who is supposedly important for some reason?

HAN SOLO: Reformed scoundrel. Always claims to save the day. Actually useless.

CHEWBACCA: Han Solo's very loud Wookiee sidekick. No match for Black Krrsantan in my opinion.

C-3PO: Simpering Triple-Zero doppelgänger.

R2-D2: Foolhardy Beetee doppelgänger.

EMPEROR PALPATINE: Our intrepid heroine's boss's boss.

BOBA FETT: Bounty hunter. Inspires fear in the hearts of all (except for our intrepid heroine).

MAZ KANATA: Badass pirate queen. Incredibly sore loser.

KORIN APHRA: Our intrepid heroine's father. Obsessed with excruciatingly boring Jedi stuff.

LONA APHRA: Our intrepid heroine's mother. Obsessed with excruciatingly boring planets.

THE ANTE: Information broker. Sometimes useful. Not to be trusted.

IG-90: Bounty hunter. Overly pedantic assassin droid. Likes to shoot things.

BOSSK: Bounty hunter. Wookiee-killing machine. Does not understand the concept of jokes.

BEEBOX: Bounty hunter. Very short, but carries a big gun.

UTANI XANE: Curator of Quarantine World III. Loves bureaucracy and crushing dreams.

SAVA TOOB-NIX: Sava of the University of Bar'leth. Hates when his lectures are interrupted (especially by our intrepid heroine).

COMMODEX TAHN: Former mortician of Naboo. All-around bad liar.

ENEB RAY: Former rebel spy. Loves to monologue.

GEONOSIAN QUEEN: Really scary. No other descriptors necessary.

STAR WARS™
DOCTOR APHRA

NARRATOR:
A long time ago, in a galaxy far, far away. . . .

CUE THEME

SCENE 1. INT. THE *ARK ANGEL.* SOMEWHERE IN THE OUTER RIM.

APHRA:
Begin recording.

APHRA (narration):
The first thing you need to know: This time I'm dead. Definitely, definitely dead.

I've *almost* died before. So many times. "More lives than a tooka-cat," that's how Sava Toob-Nix used to describe me. And this story, the one that ends with me definitely dead . . . it all starts with one of those times I *almost* died.

So let's begin there.

We hear the blasts and explosions of a truly epic space battle—perhaps a bit exaggerated in its epicness because this is the story as Aphra's telling it, and she is nothing if not over the top.

APHRA (narration):

Imagine it: the most *epic space battle* you've ever seen. Lasers! Explosions! Things that go *pew-pew*! And right in the middle of it all, our intrepid heroine—that's me!—Doctor Chelli Lona Aphra. Rogue archaeologist, weapons expert, droid reactivator extraordinaire . . . and did I mention she is also extraordinarily beautiful? Raven tresses . . . that are usually a tangled mess, because they're stuffed under a very stylish aviator cap, complete with rakish goggles. Brown eyes that spark—yes, *spark*!—with a yearning for adventure. Intriguing electro-tattoos running down her right arm—foolish, youthful mistake, or sign of an irrepressible daredevil? That's none of your business!

Let's join her as she makes her grand escape from a gang of nefarious pirates trying to gun down her glorious ship, the *Ark Angel*!

A particularly loud boom! *as Aphra's ship is hit.*

APHRA:

Dammit . . . hyperdrive down, life support hit. Okay . . . okay . . . that's fine, nothing to worry about. Activate auxiliary systems and get the crew working on it right away!

A beat as she realizes she's talking to herself.

APHRA:

Oh, right. There are no auxiliary systems. And I don't have a crew. Time to get creative . . .

The ship's comm beeps with an incoming transmission.

MAZ KANATA (on comm):

Doctor Aphra! Surrender the valuable artifacts you have stolen from us and we will leave you and your ship be and continue on our way!

Aphra speaks to Maz as she tinkers furiously with her ship's control panel, trying to buy time.

APHRA:
Heeeey, Maz Kanata! Always an honor to speak to the galaxy's most—and I mean *most*—legendary pirate queen! I can't tell you the number of times I've dreamed of this moment, just the two of us on a comm while trying to shoot each other into the Void. I can't imagine why you're shooting at li'l ol' *me*, though, I swear you've got the wrong girl—

MAZ KANATA (on comm):
Spare me your legendary—and *I* mean legendary—falsehoods, Aphra, we know you have the antique stealth microdroid dust—

APHRA:
You *wound* me with these accusations!

MAZ KANATA (on comm):
My crew went to great lengths to secure an artifact so valuable, and you, no doubt, are planning on doing something extraordinarily stupid with it—

APHRA:
What, like *use* it?

MAZ KANATA (on comm):
Exactly.

APHRA:
Okay. Now this is getting downright personal. Is there no sisterhood among rogues anymore? Tell ya what, why don't we settle in at one of those backwater holes you love so much, have a drink, talk this out like the proper ladies we are—

Another boom rocks Aphra's ship. Her tinkering gets even more furious, more desperate.

APHRA:
That was very *un*ladylike, Maz.

The Ark Angel *lets out a series of frantic beeps.*

APHRA:
Now my life support's failing, I probably only have a few breaths left in me, I'm going to die out here because you're convinced I took something from you and, worse yet, that I have some sort of nefarious *plan* for it—

MAZ KANATA (on comm):
You underestimate how well I—or anyone who's spoken to you for more than five seconds—know you.

APHRA:
Fine! *Of course* I took it! And of course I'm going to use it! You pirates think you understand the value of all these artifacts you so carelessly pilfer, but all you really understand is that they're *old,* and that means they need to be sold to a dusty old museum where they rot away into nothing. And all without ever being used for their true purpose, fulfilling their true potential—out there in the galaxy, having the extraordinary adventures they were meant for.

I mean. How would you like it if someone put *you* in a museum, Maz?

MAZ KANATA (on comm):
You are telling me that in your custody, the antique stealth microdroid dust is going to have *adventures*? Rather than merely being sold to the highest bidder?

APHRA:
Would it . . . make you stop shooting at me if that was the case?

A beat as Maz considers—or at least pretends to.

MAZ KANATA (on comm):
Probably not.

Another loud boom rocks Aphra's ship.

APHRA:
That's what I figured. And that's why . . . I also stole—er, *liberated* something else from your pirating spoils! The cutest little astro-

mech scraps . . . so shiny, and just sitting there, nestled next to the microdroid dust. I swear, they started talking to me. Wanted me to take 'em home. And I like the shiny, so I obliged.

MAZ KANATA (on comm):
[genuinely puzzled]

The . . . astromech scraps? Those were salvaged from a Corellian junkyard, but they were so rusty, so banged up and broken, even our best techs couldn't do anything with them. They're just . . . trash.

APHRA:
Yeah, I *love* trash. Watch what happens when I place my shiny new astromech bit *just so* in my central operating system.

We hear a decisive click as Aphra places the droid part in her control panel.

APHRA:
Hooks right in—'cause I've got the magic touch. Oh, and I've made so many personal modifications to the *Ark Angel,* my beloved ship will run on anything. Even old droid parts.

A loud explosion rocks Maz's ship.

MAZ KANATA (on comm):
What! Direct hit, our gravity's knocked out . . .

APHRA:
Soooo . . . did I mention that I've actually been looking for this *exact* 'mech bit? I had a theory that it would enhance my weapons system—looks like I was right! *All-purpose* astromech bits! Or at least they are in *my* hands . . .

MAZ KANATA (on comm):
I don't understand how you . . . *you* . . .

APHRA:
Your techs are a buncha charlatans, Maz. You should reaaaalllly consider replacing them if you want to keep that badass pirate queen rep.

MAZ KANATA (on comm):
That isn't . . . *Void!* Retreat! This isn't over, Aphra . . .

APHRA:
Oh, I know.

As Maz's ship retreats, Aphra actually sounds a little contemplative—

APHRA:
I really do hope we get that drink one day.

SCENE 2. INT. VAULT ROOM. QUARANTINE WORLD III. KALLIDAHIN SPACE.

Aphra stands at the entrance of the vault, gazing at the small wall safe located on the other side of the room.

Atmosphere: This facility has a rigid, very sterile quality— cavernous yet tightly secure in a way that always seems empty, despite it being full of dangerous weapons. Even the smallest sounds carry a bit of an echo, bouncing off the endless chasms and hard metal surfaces.

APHRA (narration):
Maz was right—that microdroid dust and I, we were about to have some *major* adventures together. I mean, they'd kinda have to be major if they led to my death, right?

But I'm getting ahead of myself.

My next stop, after successfully escaping Maz's pirate gang and kind of, sort of inflicting a truly astonishing amount of damage to their ship, was Quarantine World III in Kallidahin space.

This quarantine world was established to, and I quote from some really boring academic text I only partially skimmed at university, "safely contain artifacts classified as highly dangerous and possibly lethal."

In my professional archaeologist opinion . . . this is a buncha bantha crap.

The things contained in this facility are deadly works of *art*. They should be out in the world, being truly appreciated by those who understand their power. They should be living their dreams and blowing stuff up.

If I had the time—and, let's face it, if someone was paying me an astronomical amount of credits—I'd liberate every single artifact in this quarantine world's cold, gray central facility, with its maze of twisting wires, its middling surveillance system, and its overwhelming feeling of excruciatingly dull . . . emptiness.

But I had to focus: I was only here for one thing.

Bypassing surveillance was no problem. Ditto breaking into the cavernous vault housing the thing I was after.

Admirers of my many exploits often ask me: What is it with you and breaking into things? How do you do it so fast, and with such precision? Is that something you learned at university?

No, of course not. Sava Toob-Nix's head—hell, maybe his entire body—would explode at the mere *thought* of a student crediting her incredible safecracking skills to his teachings.

The truth is, mechanical things *speak* to me. Droids. Ships. Vaults containing valuable instruments of destruction. The satisfying click of a gear sliding into place or a wire detaching in just the right spot . . . it's like a language only I can understand. I feel these words that aren't quite words deep in my bones, the way I imagine a musician hears the opening notes of their masterpiece symphony.

And I use my understanding of this language to fix things. And also to break things.

Okay, *mostly* to break things.

Standing at the entrance of the massive vault I'd just successfully broken into, I gazed at my nemesis, buried deep inside. It was positioned on the wall farthest from me, on the other end of a long metal bridge, and it had a glowing, green cast to it. It looked like some kind of super-creepy *eye thing* that could see right through me. It was . . .

Ugh. It was *another* vault.

Well, more like a safe. Smaller, but still yet another thing I'd have to break into.

APHRA:
Hmm. Surveillance already bypassed. Guns, but no visible triggers. Just an empty room.

[big sarcasm]

Perfectly safe to walk across, I'm sure.

This is where my new and extremely talented little friend, Mr. Stealth Antique Microdroid Dust, comes in.

Bit of a mouthful, that name. Sir, may I simply call you . . . Stealthy?

[beat]

Okay, then, Stealthy: Let's go on that adventure—time to see what you can do!

Aphra blows the dust across the room, igniting a web of red laser-beam-like triggers.

APHRA:
Annnnnnd . . . looks like we got a whole mess of glowing red laser things that are actually highly sensitive security triggers. Good job, Mr. Stealthy!

Okay . . . no problem. I'll crawl under them. Go around them. Turn myself into microdroid dust and float over them, all superior-like.

Safe, if you can hear me: You will be mine.

APHRA (narration):
When there's no door in sight, I find one. When I can't find one, I *make* one. Kinda like I did with ol' Maz back there. I used all the stuff I stole—er, *liberated*—from her to make my own door.

I slid to the floor, crawling on my belly, avoiding the bright-red beams of light that would surely lead to my doom if I made contact with them. Well, mostly they'd lead to me getting caught by the uptight, holier-than-thou security that runs this joint, but whatever.

Imagine if one of these laser things did, like, vivisect me, though. That would at least be an exciting way to go, right? Maybe Sava Toob-Nix's new students would read about *me* in one of their boring academic texts!

[affects a pretentious, professorial-type voice]

And that was the last adventure for legendary archaeologist Doctor Chelli Lona Aphra, who we don't even *really* need to name since you all know who she is already! She overcame a hardscrabble, boring-as-dirt past to become one of the galaxy's leading experts on highly sought-after artifacts, dodged death oh-so-many times . . . and was finally murdered by a rogue laser beam when she belly-crawled just a little too far to the left—

[normal voice]

Hmm. Actually, that doesn't sound very impressive, does it?

I know you were probably hoping *this* was the moment I died for real, which would make our story very short. And everyone who wants me dead would be able to celebrate.

I . . . think it'd be a pretty big celebration.

Sorry, intrepid space enemies, no such luck. Mr. Stealthy made sure I avoided all those pesky lasers, and I finally reached the creepy glowing-eye safe, my hand clapping against one of those boring gray walls with relief.

A few more milliseconds and I got the safe open . . .

The safe pops open, revealing the Triple-Zero Matrix hidden inside—a small control panel of twisting wires and glowing lights.

APHRA (narration):
And there it was. The thing I'd come for. The climax of my totally brilliant plan that was totally going to make me a whole lot of money. A glorious tiny control pad of lights and wires containing one of the most dangerous things in the entire galaxy.

APHRA:
Well, hello, Triple-Zero Personality Matrix. You are looking *delightful* this evening.

APHRA (narration):
The Triple-Zero Matrix was another thing that just *spoke* to me. As I disconnected it from its cold, soulless prison, I swore I felt it perk up—its lights flashed more insistently, its constant hum of power grew more vigorous. It knew that wherever it was going *had* to be more exciting than a musty old vault.

I took a moment to gaze at it, admiration swelling in my chest: This tiny rectangle of crossed wires probably wouldn't look impressive to anyone else.

But *I* knew: I was holding the most dangerous thing in the galaxy.

Now I had to get out of this sad, silent quarantine world. And then it was time for one of my favorite parts: getting paid.

Same drill as before, only in reverse. Slide to the floor, belly-crawl, avoid those triggers . . .

APHRA:
Careful . . . careful . . . Keep your head down and your elbows in . . . Don't bump the laser, don't end up a footnote in a musty academic text . . .

Aphra's elbow bumps one of the triggers, setting off a loud alarm.

APHRA:
Oh, son of a . . . *Traitorous elbow!* How dare you!

Lasers shoot at Aphra, and the alarm gets even louder.

APHRA (narration):
Yeah, I bumped the stupid laser. I didn't die—it just stung a little. I leapt to my feet, forgoing all attempts at stealth or delicacy—and I ran.

SCENE 3. INT. CORRIDOR. QUARANTINE WORLD III. KALLIDAHIN SPACE. MOMENTS LATER.

Aphra sprints through the corridor of the facility, ducking to avoid the many things shooting at her.

Atmosphere: Now the facility feels like it's come to life, its security systems deployed! We should still get that cavernous feeling, but things are less sterile and way more chaotic—just the way Aphra likes them.

APHRA (narration):
As I sprinted through the corridor—which, by the way, was as boring and gray as the rest of the quarantine facility, I guess they don't want you getting distracted by anything *actually interesting* while you're running for your life—I remembered something else I didn't learn from one of those texts I didn't read: Never look behind you.

Because when I spared a glance over my shoulder, I saw that—in addition to all the facility munitions trying to shoot me back to the

Outer Rim—someone had kindly dispatched a shielded destroyer droid to chase me!

The droid clanks after Aphra, its speed increasing as it bears down on her.

APHRA:
Oh, *double* son of a—

The clanking gets faster and faster as the droid pursues Aphra. Her breathing and footfalls speed up. In the distance, we hear the rumble of a large bay door closing.

APHRA (narration):
I ran with all my might toward the hangar, increasing my speed as the bay door lowered shut, the clanking of the destroyer getting closer . . . and *closer* . . .

I'll confess, I was dying to stop, turn, and really inspect that droid. Was it just me, or was its clank extra loud, especially considering that it was shielded? Was its lower joint mechanism rusty? Did it have a rotting secondhand part? Did it just need a little oil?

That mechanical language was pinging through my brain again— I could fix it, if given the chance . . .

But, no. There were other things I had to worry about.

I flung myself at the bay door, skidding along the floor, hands outstretched . . . just a few seconds, perfectly timed, and I'd make it, I'd make it, I'd *definitely* make it . . .

Aphra slams into the bay door with a massive crash.

APHRA:
Gaaaaaahhhh . . . *dammit.*

APHRA (narration):
Annnnd . . . I didn't make it. Slammed into the bay door just as it hit the floor. Perfect.

I rolled onto my side and wheezed for breath, the wind knocked out of me. Even though I was seeing stars, I brushed my fingertips along the bay door. Just to make sure it was *really* closed.

Yeah . . . it was. Cutting me off from the *Ark Angel,* from escape, from . . . everything.

And from liberating the Triple-Zero Matrix from this godsawful place.

I *had* to find another door.

UTANI XANE:
Doctor Aphra! You are an irresponsible and troublesome woman.

Utani Xane and his gang of security droids surround Aphra.

APHRA:
[sotto]

Great, the really boring cavalry's here.

[regular voice]

Heeeey, Utani Xane. And . . . uh, friends. Security droids? Sirs, madams? Not sure what you prefer.

UTANI XANE:
Silence!

APHRA:
Utani Xane, so nice to see an old . . . friend. I didn't know you were working here. Why am I not surprised?

UTANI XANE:
I'm equally unsurprised to find you setting off the alarms. There's a *reason* why the Triple-Zero Matrix has been quarantined for *centuries.*

APHRA:
Yes, because of people like *you*! Small minds who just want to hide beautiful things in storage or a museum.

It should be in an armory!

UTANI XANE:
And you should be in prison again. Maybe this time, it'll stick.

APHRA (narration):
The overzealous security droids clamped binders on me and took my treasure, but I was already thinking of all the ways I would obviously foil them and escape in a blaze of glory. Loud, explosive, all-blasters-firing glory.

It'd been pretty explosive the last time I'd encountered Utani Xane, too—he used to be the curator at a bustling museum on Coruscant, specializing in outdated droid artifacts salvaged after the Clone Wars. I applied for a job there—I know, I know. You're thinking, *Really, Chelli? When did you ever apply for a proper job? Is it Opposite Day? Or, more precisely, The Antithesis of Everything You Are and Will Ever Be Day?*

Look, I was in a bit of a dry spell after splitting with some contentious associates who'd helped me raid a . . . *mostly* abandoned fortress on Sarjenn Prime. I thought it might be nice to rack up credits and get an official-like title under my belt—assistant curator—because even the lowlifes who hire for the semi-illicit type jobs I do are impressed by such things. I figured Xane would be so dazzled by my expertise, I'd be promoted to the top in no time!

Head Curator Aphra, in charge of absolutely everything! Has a nice ring to it, eh? For a fleeting moment, I was almost . . . *respectable*!

Buuuuuut . . . turns out folks like Utani Xane—sniveling little bureaucrats with fancy titles and certain ideas about how things "should" be done—really don't like it when their underlings take initiative.

I couldn't help it. Being surrounded by all those supposedly outdated droid parts . . . well, they started talking to me in that irresistible mechanical language, and I simply *had* to respond.

All I did was put a few of those old droid pieces together and reactivate the whole shebang. You know, so instead of dusty old parts, we'd have a full-on *working* mega-droid, built from seemingly disparate bits but put together by a genius—that's me!—who's able to think outside the box. Don't you think a *mega-droid* would have been way more exciting for the museum patrons to take a gander at?

See? *Initiative.*

Utani Xane didn't view it that way. Can you believe he not only fired me, he tried to have me *arrested*?

Okay, so. This wasn't *just* because I built a mega-droid . . . the mega-droid also went on a total rampage that I hadn't predicted and almost crushed Utani Xane *and* a few of the wealthier museum patrons and . . . well. Let's just say the museum would have needed a fortune in repairs in order to reopen. Actually, they would have had to build a whole new museum.

Xane lost his post, obviously. And now he was here to bother me again.

His face was unreadable as he examined the Triple-Zero Matrix, his clumsy fingers mishandling the delicate artifact in a way that made me want to scream.

If Triple-Zero could've spoken right then, I bet he'd be screaming, too. Because he'd know this annoying bureaucrat was about to imprison him.

But then, an unexpected twist . . .

SECURITY DROID:
Curator Utani Xane . . . incoming TIE fighter.

APHRA (narration):
It was time to take some *initiative* again . . .

SCENE 4. INT. CORRIDOR. QUARANTINE WORLD III.
KALLIDAHIN SPACE. MOMENTS LATER.

APHRA (narration):
Ahhh, the glorious feeling of *disruption*. For a few moments, Utani Xane and his goons scrambled to figure out what was happening. Who was on that TIE fighter? And why were they here?

I didn't know and I didn't care, but I was sure of one thing— somehow all this chaos was going to give me the chance to escape!

UTANI XANE:
The vessel hasn't communicated at all? No clearance codes? This is most displeasing . . .

SECURITY DROID:
Apologies, Curator. We have no scheduled visitors, deliveries, or—

UTANI XANE:
Then *who* . . .

The ominous sound of Darth Vader's breathing echoes down the corridor . . .

UTANI XANE:
[flustered—but also a bit scared]

L-lord Vader! This is a quarantined world. Treaties clearly state—

DARTH VADER:
Enough.

APHRA (narration):
Whoa! "Lord Vader" as in the one and only Darth Vader? I'd thought he was a myth, a bogeyman parents used to get their unruly younglings to behave.

As someone who regularly fights death and wins, he'd never sounded *that* scary to me, but even I had to admit: He cut a pretty intimidating figure in all that ominous black armor, striding toward Utani Xane with purpose. Personally, I thought the cape was *a bit much,* but hey—you don't attain bogeyman status with tastefully understated costuming.

Naturally, my first thought was:

Oh, hey, he exists! And he knows how to make an entrance. I should ask if he has access to any of those super-dangerous, possibly mythical Sith artifacts I keep hearing about, right? I mean. Those are probably worth endless *credits! No, no . . . focus, Aphra.*

Anyway, his dark lordliness didn't listen to any of Utani Xane's blather. He just raised a hand and did one of those Force woo-woo magic things, sending the annoying security droids flying!

The security droids clatter across the floor.

UTANI XANE:
Lord Vader!

Vader draws his lightsaber.

DARTH VADER:
I said . . . *enough.*

The security droids fire on Vader. He easily deflects their blasts with his lightsaber. The sounds of intense battle continue as Aphra narrates . . .

APHRA (narration):
The security droids fired on Vader, but he easily deflected all of their pathetic blasts with his lightsaber.

While the boys were fighting it out and Utani Xane was trying to weasel his weasel-y little ass to an escape pod, I picked the lock on my binders, freeing my hands. Then I flung my body right under Utani Xane, tripping him.

Because of course he was *also* trying to weasel away with my precious cargo: Triple-Zero, which he'd barely shown any interest in while I was going on and on about its many incredible attributes.

Why do people try to steal things they don't appreciate?

I scuffled with him, making a desperate grab for the Matrix . . .

APHRA:
Gimme that!

As Aphra and Utani Xane scuffle, the Matrix goes flying from Utani Xane's grasp.

APHRA (narration):
Of course he dropped it. *Of course.*

And of course it was right at this moment that I noticed we had scuffled our way to the very end of a massive ledge, right above one of the quarantine facility's gray, echoey chasms.

The Matrix bounced once, twice, both of us trying to grab it—then it tumbled over the ledge.

APHRA:
Oh no!

APHRA (narration):
And of course I dove after it. *Of course.*

Some would say this is because I'm a daredevil hothead with no self-preservation skills. I prefer to say it's because I'm *focused.* On completing my mission or whatever.

Listen, Utani Xane, I may not have been good enough to be your precious assistant curator . . . but I know how to get stuff *done.*

I went flying over the ledge, adrenaline pumping through my every cell. And then I was suspended in the air, looking down at the unending darkness of the chasm below.

Come to think of it, this was another moment where I almost died.

But honestly, I didn't care. I was focused only on getting that Matrix into my hot little hand. One of my arms shot out to grasp the ledge, saving me from falling into that endless chasm forever.

The other hand was all I needed to grasp the Matrix. I felt my fingertips closing around it, triumph surging through my entire body.

APHRA:
Gotcha.

APHRA (narration):
For a moment, that triumph was all I needed. Then it slowly dawned on me that I *also* needed to figure out how to climb back to safety.

Thankfully, Mr. Darth Vader saved me, or I'd probably still be hanging from that blasted ledge, dangling over a death drop.

He'd slashed his way through all the security droids. Now he advanced on Utani Xane, stabbing him unceremoniously in the back with his lightsaber.

UTANI XANE:
Gukk!

APHRA (narration):
Honestly, it's better than what that little worm deserved.

You liked being the big, bad curator—eh, Xane? Lording your power and narrow-minded thoughts over me like I was a bug, a mindless drone assigned to do your bidding and nothing more.

Well, I guess now you can *curate your own death.*

[beat]

Sorry. That sounded better in my head. Note to recording: Let's consider deleting that part later.

Vader gazed at me, hanging off the ledge, the Matrix still clutched protectively in my free hand.

DARTH VADER:
Doctor Aphra. I have need of you.

APHRA (narration):
I know, right? Darth Vader—his lordliness, feared throughout the galaxy, just straight up murdered Utani Xane without a second thought—came here for *me*? Probably most people would have let go of that rickety ledge thing and taken their chances with a very long plunge to a most certainly painful death.

But I'm not most people.

He extended a hand.

I took it.

There was my door.

A beat as Aphra tries to let the momentousness of this sink in for us . . .

APHRA (narration):
Wait, *wait.* This was a *big* moment. I need you to really understand the . . . the *epicness.* The majesty. Let's try that again.

Recording: Overwrite that last bit with *this* bit. I mean, if you think it sounds better.

Eh. Keep both bits and let me decide later!

Okay, let's do this . . .

Aphra clears her throat theatrically, then starts over with more panache.

APHRA (narration):
But I'm not most people.

He extended a hand.

I took it.

And then I totally gave a speech!

APHRA:
Lord Vader, I, Doctor Aphra—rogue archaeologist, initiative-taking genius, definitely too good to be assistant curator to someone as blah as Utani Xane—

UTANI XANE:
[dramatic death choke]

Crooooooaaaaaaaak . . .

APHRA:
Silence, Utani Xane, you dying worm! Lord Vader, I accept your amazing offer—whatever it is—and am pleased to be at your service!

A weighted beat of Vader's breathing.

APHRA (narration):
He didn't say anything. As I'd learn, he *often* didn't say anything. But as he stared back at me with those dark, empty pits—the eyes of his helmet . . . I just *knew* this was the beginning of the most important partnership of my life.

Because while I'm used to finding my door, I immediately sensed that this one . . . was different. He was powerful, he was ruthless, and if I stood in his way, he'd kill me without a second thought.

And that meant this was the biggest opportunity to come my way in . . . well. Possibly *ever*.

If I could figure out how to play this potentially deadly situation—and this definitely deadly son of the Empire—*just right* . . . I knew I'd have a shot at more riches and adventure and glory than I'd ever dreamed of.

Past Aphra was definitely thinking way too small, trying to pilfer bits and bobs from space scavengers and running errands for the Droid Gotra.

Now I was on the brink of something *massive*. All I had to do was gain the bogeyman's trust, learn every single weakness lurking underneath that forbidding armor . . . and then use those things to my advantage.

Sure, no problem. All in a day's work.

SCENE 5. INT. THE *ARK ANGEL*. LATER.

Aphra leads Vader into the nook in the Ark Angel *where she keeps all her droid tinkering projects.*

Atmosphere: In direct contrast with the sterile quarantine facility, the Ark Angel *should sound more grubby—the ship is always settling, creaking, whirring with random beeps and blips from Aphra's projects. All part of Aphra's customization and her tendency to hoard droids and other mechanical bits. It feels very lived-in—her version of homey.*

APHRA (narration):
Okay, honestly: The "man of few words" thing was cool, but it also meant I had no idea what Vader wanted. I brought him on board the *Ark Angel* and prayed to all the deities I don't believe in that I wasn't making a major faux pas in Sith Lord etiquette. I wanted him to feel like I was on his side—even though the only side I'm ever on is mine.

I mean. What are you supposed to do when such a dangerous personage decides to bless your home with his presence? I basically built the *Ark Angel* from the ground up and I love my baby very much—especially since I've upgraded and modified and improved the ship's systems to my exact liking. But . . . Darth Vader seemed like the type who was used to much fancier digs. And there wasn't any time to tidy up or put out tea and cookies.

Wait, does Darth Vader eat tea and cookies?

Does Darth Vader *eat,* period?

My father had told me all kinds of stories about the Sith—his main focus had been moldy old Jedi artifacts, but I'd always been more fascinated by his tales of the dark side. Long-lost Sith artifacts were generally characterized as more . . . *destructive.* Deadly. Bringers of chaos. In other words, they were at the cross section of so many of my interests! And there was always gossip flying around in archaeological circles about where to find them . . . if they actually existed . . .

I had *so many questions* I wanted to ask the Dark Lord, but after witnessing his treatment of Utani Xane, I thought it prudent to keep those to myself for now.

Yes, that's right—I just described a decision I made as "prudent." Try to contain your shock.

I led Vader to the area of my ship where I keep a lot of my droid projects, tinkerings, works-in-progress . . . and tried to play it by ear.

APHRA:
Welcome aboard the *Ark Angel,* Sir Darth Vader. Big fan. Huge!

How can I help?

DARTH VADER:
This is private business. I recently destroyed some of your reactivated droids. They impressed me.

APHRA:
Thank you, Mr. Lord Vader.

Uh, sir? Your majesty? Your illustriousness?

Honestly, no idea what to call you. I'm a rogue archaeologist, not a protocol droid. Getting the right protocol droid is the reason I was here.

How did you find me, anyway?

A weighted beat of Vader's ominous breathing.

APHRA:
Actually . . . I don't want to know, do I?

APHRA (narration):
Wow, I was playing it *so* cool. But inside, there was this fluttery-jittery thing happening in my stomach—most people would probably call that thing fear.

I call it *excitement.*

I love the beginning of this kind of puzzle. Gathering all those observations and tiny bits of information about someone, filing them away for later—to be deployed exactly when you can use them.

I didn't want his lordliness to know what I was thinking, of course—he didn't need to know that my brain was working overtime, whirring away like one of my beloved mechanical contraptions.

Luckily I am a total master at acting like nothing matters—especially when something really, *really* does.

So I kept going through the motions of what I was planning to do next anyway. I downloaded the Triple-Zero Matrix into the *Ark Angel*'s main computer, offering Mr. Vader my ever-entertaining commentary so he wouldn't think I was trying to, like, *escape* or something.

APHRA:
This is the Triple-Zero Protocol Personality Matrix. Had a few bugs. Twitchy coupling. Neurocybernetic glitches. Tendency to drain organics to collect their blood. That kind of thing.

But it speaks languages that no one else does, and that's what I need . . .

Problem is that it's code-locked. I'll need a few hours to break in, so I can set that to work, and then see what I can do to help you . . .

Vader taps on a keyboard next to Aphra's main computer.

APHRA:
What are you doing?

APHRA (narration):
Okay, so that was *not quite* playing it cool, but his dark lordliness just started typing away on my control panel! On my precious ship! I whirled back to my screen, prepared to give him a piece of my mind for messing with such a delicate treasure. But then . . .

APHRA:
You've . . . unlocked it. You unlocked the *Triple-Zero Matrix.* You didn't have the codes. How . . . how did you do that?

APHRA (narration):
Of course he didn't answer. And as I'd come to learn . . . it was usually better when he didn't. I tried to hide my shock and went back to my whole "going through the motions" thing, pulling out a handy protocol droid body—something I'd stolen, er, taken with me when I'd fought my way out of Coruscant, Utani Xane's loathsome security detail hot on my tail. I'd decided it was a perfectly reasonable severance, especially since Xane had basically fired me with no fair warning.

APHRA:
Now the Triple-Zero Matrix is ready to take up a brand-spankin'-new home in this boy's body. And much sooner than I expected. It's like, dare I say . . . a *mega-droid*?

APHRA (narration):
Oof. Okay, that was a slight miscalculation. What was I expecting, that he'd *laugh*? I dunno, I guess I thought, *here's* someone who would've been totally into my droid-combining experiments! I was still in intel-gathering mode, figuring out what made the guy tick.

APHRA:
S-sorry. It's just . . . You . . . are even more interesting than I could have hoped, Sir Vader.

DARTH VADER:
Lord Vader. Continue.

APHRA:
Okay. Give me a second to get this installed . . .

APHRA (narration):
I slid the Matrix into the protocol droid's head—and there it was, that satisfying click into place. My beautiful mechanical language. For a moment, Lord Vader and the *Ark Angel* melted away, and it was just me, the droid, and those secret words that aren't words.

I knew my boy was going to wake up.

And I knew he was going to be magnificent.

Triple-Zero's eyes light up, glowing red.

TRIPLE-ZERO:
Oh, hello.

I am 0-0-0 or Triple-Zero, if you prefer. I'm a protocol droid, specialized in etiquette, customs, translation, and torture, ma'am.

Charmed to meet you, I'm sure.

May I shake your hand, in the polite manner of organics?

Triple-Zero holds a hand out to Aphra, as if for a friendly shake.

APHRA:
Nice try, Trip, but I already know you better than that, and I *know* how you feel about "organics."

TRIPLE-ZERO:
Madam, I am not sure what you mean! I live to serve you blood-filled sacks of flesh, and have nothing but the utmost respect for—

APHRA:

[interrupts]

Override: Imprint "master" on all individuals present. Codename: Aphra and Codename: Vader.

TRIPLE-ZERO:

Ah, better not shake hands, then, Mistress Aphra. May route a fatal shock through my palm. Old habits die hard and all that. And in my experience, they certainly die harder than most organics, ma'am.

As there's no one here to murder, presently, how may I be of assistance?

APHRA:

Awww, all this murder talk. You really know how to charm a girl—a girl who happens to be a blood-filled sack of flesh. I actually have a *non*-murder task for you. In fact, it involves the opposite: I need you to bring something to *life*.

Here we go . . .

Aphra pulls out a blastomech droid.

APHRA (narration):

Yeah, so I had a little project for my new friend Trip in the form of a "blastomech" droid prototype—how did I liberate such a rare and destructive thing, you ask? You thought blastomechs were a *myth*, you say? Well, that's another story . . .

The recording goes fuzzy.

APHRA (narration):

Hmm, never mind. Recording: Delete that last part. Some great adventures are best left *mysterious*. Also, dear listener, I don't trust you to not immediately turn this recording over to certain annoying authorities and there are things about that particular great adventure they *definitely* don't need to know.

Anyway, I love blastomechs because they're so *cute*—squat, domed, rolling around on their little wheels. They look like *astro-*

mechs. But when you really get to know them . . . well, they pack a major punch.

Maybe I feel a kinship with them. Some people have also described *me* as "cute."

They have no idea.

APHRA:
Here's your first official task for your new master, Triple-Zero. I need you to tell this boy to wake up.

TRIPLE-ZERO:
All this effort for a simple astromech?

APHRA:
Not exactly. This is BT-1, a blastomech prototype. Does enough to pass as an astro. But it's primarily a cover. It's a specialized assassin droid. Sadly, it's entirely homicidal.

TRIPLE-ZERO:
Is *sadly* really the word we're looking for here, Mistress Aphra? That sounds like a highly desirable quality to me!

APHRA:
Hmm. I guess it all depends on your perspective, Trip!

DARTH VADER:
My patience is wearing thin, Doctor.

APHRA:
Right. Sorry, your lordliness: This li'l old blastomech wiped out its Tarkin Initiative base before setting the place to self-destruct and jettisoning itself into space.

TRIPLE-ZERO:
A true warrior . . .

APHRA:
I'm already appreciating your unique take on things, Triple-Zero.

I . . . um, *found* it, fitted it with some stronger behavioral inhibitors, but can't get it to wake up. Its core identity only speaks the R&D language of the base—

DARTH VADER:

And the base is no more.

APHRA:

Exactly, sir. But Trip, here—I think he can fix this boy right up for me. Er, for *us*.

TRIPLE-ZERO:

Ah, I see! I was also a product of the good Sir Tarkin's Initiative, and so am entirely fluent with all internal test languages. That is a wonderful plan, Mistress Aphra!

APHRA:

Then get this dumpy gunboy up and about.

TRIPLE-ZERO:

Ahem, allow me to access the correct language processor . . .

BLEEP! BLEEP BLEEP!

Beetee whirs to life.

BEETEE:

BLEEP! BLEEP BLEEP BLEEP!

Beetee arms himself, weapons engaging and unfolding, flames shooting from his ports.

APHRA (narration):

What did I just say about loving blastomechs? Maybe I should take that back. Because as soon as this wee homicidal maniac whirred to life, his first action was to deploy his many, *many* weapons— they unfurled from every part of him like he was some kind of fancy rebel army knife.

And then he started shooting *flames* out of his little ports . . .

TRIPLE-ZERO:
No, BT-1! No, you can't possibly do that! They are our masters!

Vader draws his lightsaber.

TRIPLE-ZERO:
Also, who would clean up the mess?

APHRA (narration):
Well . . . great. Murderous droid, meet murderous lord of the Empire. Lucky for me and my ship, Triple-Zero managed to have a serious bonding moment with Beetee . . . or at least that's what I assume happened, because after Trip blurted out all that nonsense, my dearest deadly blastomech disengaged his weapons and powered down. At least for the moment.

Leaving *me* to bond with his lordliness!

I slid to the floor, drew my knees to my chest, and let my head rest on my folded arms.

I'd had a *day.*

APHRA:
Well. That's another activation survived.

But who am I talking to? This must be a quiet day for you, Lord Vader. Fitting in a meeting with me before getting back to your busy schedule of applying a jackboot to the throat of the young rebels, eh?

DARTH VADER:
You are . . . *overly fond* of speaking.

APHRA:
I'm nervous. I make my living reactivating weapons like this pair . . . and *you* make me nervous. There's something about tall, dark, and able-to-kill-me guys that make a girl nervous.

What do you want from me?

DARTH VADER:

There was a time when I had armies at my beck and call. That time has passed. I need resources of my own. *Private* resources.

APHRA (narration):

I'd heard the gossip, of course—that Vader had been . . . not exactly disgraced. But definitely *demoted* within the Empire after the rebels destroyed the Death Star. But, y'know, he's *Darth Vader*. I just assumed that . . . well, if he even existed, something like that was a temporary setback, like getting detention, and he'd be back to full dark lordliness in no time.

But from what he was saying, that didn't seem to be the case. It sounded like the Emperor had demoted him *hard*—I sensed a thread of humiliation in his voice that was all too familiar. It was the same humiliation I'd felt when Utani Xane had destroyed any chance I had at a "respectable" career and/or title.

I didn't even *want* the title.

And I never wanted to be "respectable."

But . . . I *did* want people to understand that I was—I *am*—the best at what I do. Brilliant, innovative, genius. That me reassembling and reactivating my mega-droid into something all new and different and *better* wasn't a failure. It was a *triumph*.

Vader, I sensed, needed a triumph of his own. He needed to show all those pinheaded bureaucrats that he could be *great* again.

He was looking to restore his power, and he was taking *initiative*.

I could *so* use that.

Like I said, I can always tell when an opportunity's about to happen.

I grabbed on to it with both hands.

APHRA:

Lord Vader, I was . . . abstractly meant to be delivering these two droids to the Droid Gotra. They had another mission lined up . . . but *you're* my next mission, aren't you? And the next. And the next.

DARTH VADER:
Doctor—

APHRA:
Sorry, I'm just so . . . *excited*. You're what I've been looking for all my life.

Whoa. That just gave me shivers.

These droids are yours now. What else do you need?

DARTH VADER:
I need troops of unquestioning loyalty.

APHRA:
Hey, I understand. Who wouldn't want a phalanx of carefully restored battle droids? I know where to find them. The Droid Gotra wanted me to recover an . . . unusual droid factory. It's under close watch by you Imperials—plus not-exactly-friendly locals.

DARTH VADER:
This will not be a problem. And Doctor Aphra: It should go without saying that I require *discretion* in this matter.

APHRA:
Of course, of course. Discretion is my middle name. Sooo . . . how do you feel about a secret mission to Geonosis, Lord Vader?

A beat of Vader's breathing.

DARTH VADER:
I have no feelings regarding Geonosis.

APHRA:
Good. Then we need to move. I won't let you down.

DARTH VADER:
Wise, Aphra. That would be a mistake.

APHRA (narration):
I know what you're thinking. It was just *so easy* for Doctor Aphra, that lovable, morally bankrupt scoundrel, to switch her allegiance

to the Dark Lord Vader . . . but does she have an endgame here? Patience, dear listener. I needed to finish gathering intel before I could form a brilliant plan. And my *most* brilliant plans usually don't reveal themselves until the very last second.

For now, I was in survival mode—knock out what's right in front of you, extinguish the most immediate fire, and keep the ol' brain whirring.

I'd taken Vader's hand, in part, because the only other option was plunging to a messy, embarrassing, decidedly *non*-epic death—and I've been avoiding deaths of the non-epic kind all my life.

But listen, there was more to it than that. Because here's the first valuable bit of intel I was able to gather.

Of all the people in all the galaxy, Vader sought *me* out. He recognized my skills. My talents. My potential for *greatness.*

Almost no one else saw that in me. Not my mother, who carted me off to some desolate wasteland of a rotting space-rock to keep me out of so-called danger. Not my professors at university, who thought my methods were all flash, nothing more. Not Utani Xane, who fired me for trying to do something *great.* And *certainly* not . . .

Well. A lot of people.

But Vader *saw* me. He was maybe the first person to *truly* see me—and everything I could do.

Okay, maybe not *everything.* Because if he'd been able to see deep into the innermost workings of my brain, he'd have known I wasn't *really* on his team, no matter how many simpering honorifics I threw his way.

Again: The only team I care about is Team Me.

And Team Me knew this was the chance of a lifetime. Whether I was dangling off a ledge in a drafty quarantine world or activating a droid that could shoot fire out of its nether regions . . . whenever Darth Vader offered me that hand, I'd take it.

So as I got to my feet and took the helm of my ship, setting a course for Geonosis, I kept watching him, looking for those telltale weaknesses.

I'd find them eventually. I always do.

SCENE 6. EXT. UNIVERSITY OF BAR'LETH. DAY. FLASHBACK.

APHRA (narration):
The Dark Lord had really stressed that *discretion* bit. And . . . well, okay, maybe that's not *exactly* one of the things I'm known for, but trust me: I know how to do *stealth*. In fact, I think my reputation for being all flashy and adventurous, the kind of girl who explosions just seem to follow around . . . *enhances* my ability to be stealthy. People get comfortable in their assumptions about who I am, and before they know what's happening, I've tricked them into giving me whatever I want.

I mean, take Sava Toob-Nix.

That crusty old geezer attained his position as sava of the University of Bar'leth—my not-so-esteemed alma mater—through lying and trickery. Normally, those are qualities I respect, but Toob-Nix was such a sour-faced stick-in-the-mud, I pretty much hated him on sight.

And unlucky for me, the feeling was mutual.

We got off on the wrong foot immediately.

I'd just started my doctorate program, and I was running late to one of Toob-Nix's frightfully dull lectures on best archiving practices. I wasn't late on purpose; a second-year I'd been having on-and-off relations with found out about the third-year I was *also* having on-and-off relations with and apparently neither of them knew about the "off" part. It was *drama,* there was lots of yelling, and neither of them seemed sympathetic when I explained that it's not my fault I'm so damn irresistible.

Anyway, Sava Toob-Nix had already warned me that if I was late again, he'd get the ol' expulsion process started. At that point, I had next to nothing—I still thought university was the way to a proper professional life, I hadn't yet perfected my own brilliant archaeological methods, and I didn't always know how to find that door.

But I did know how to find a *window.*

So that day, when I was about to be late and Sava Toob-Nix locked me out of the lecture hall, I very *stealthily* shimmied my way through the window in the back and was slinking to my seat. I'd *almost* made it . . . but of course, right before I did . . . the sava just *had* to let loose with one of his terrible opinions.

SAVA TOOB-NIX:
—and unfortunately, one of our greatest academic facilities, the university library on the Fifth Moon of Thrinittik, is no more. It once housed some of the most important artifacts in the galaxy—sadly, they were not preserved properly, or they might have survived the cataclysmic blast that destroyed the entire structure and everything in it—

APHRA:
[blurt]

That's not true!

SAVA TOOB-NIX:
Chelli Lona Aphra! What have I told you about being late and disruptive—

APHRA:

But . . . I just . . . what you're saying *isn't true.* Yes, the university library on the Fifth Moon of Thrinittik was attacked, and some of it did crumble into dust. But pieces of the structure are still standing, and those artifacts . . . well, some of them are likely just buried deep in the ground, waiting for someone to find them. A particularly enterprising team could take initiative, and—

SAVA TOOB-NIX:

And . . . what? Get themselves killed chasing after fairy tales? Such an expedition would never be authorized—

APHRA:

Isn't that all the more reason to do it? Isn't that what being an archaeologist is about? Making new discoveries, finding treasures of the past, being able to see the . . . the fullness of the history of the entire galaxy? If we want to make *real* discoveries, it's always going to be a little dangerous—

SAVA TOOB-NIX:

What insolence! I've had a bad feeling about you since I first saw your impertinent face, Aphra. If you're going to contradict your professors and promote these . . . these *dangerous* ideas about unsanctioned expeditions, well, you won't be doing it here—

SANA STARROS:

She's right.

SAVA TOOB-NIX:

Excuse me?

SANA STARROS:

I said, she's right.

APHRA (narration):

Oh, who's that smoky voice? Mmm, sounds like Corellian whiskey, burning down your throat.

That, dear listener, is Sana Starros. And I kind of wish I'd never met her.

But in the moment . . . I was temporarily dazzled. She always looked so . . . *neat*. So put together. Clothes perfectly pressed, never a wrinkle on her. Her dark-brown skin was luminous, her gaze was piercing, and her flowing, perfectly styled mane of midnight tresses was positively *regal*.

In other words, she was my total opposite. I was always chaos, a mess—that day, my clothes and my hair and . . . well, my *everything* were disheveled and rumpled, thanks to the hasty way I'd exited my three-way lovers' quarrel.

I'm not sure how I'd never noticed her before—perhaps it was because she didn't speak up that often in class. And she certainly never *disrupted* class. She was stoic and serious, a model pupil. But when she finally spoke that day . . . whoo, boy. That *voice*.

Also, she was taking my side, which is one of the most attractive qualities a human being can possess.

SAVA TOOB-NIX:
Sana Starros! Explain yourself!

SANA STARROS:
There's research in the logs of the old Maseonna Collective—the archaeological think tank?—showing that the library wasn't completely destroyed, and positing that the artifacts still exist. You'd just have to *really* dig to find them.

APHRA:
Yeah, like I said . . .

SANA STARROS:
And it would be an unsanctioned expedition. But not impossible.

SAVA TOOB-NIX:
Well, I . . . I . . .

SANA STARROS:
I'm just saying, sir. The research that these artifacts survived exists in logs that can be found on this very campus—it's just a little obscure.

APHRA:

Not so obscure that a *sava* should be totally ignorant of it—

SANA STARROS:

I'm sure Sava Toob-Nix just hasn't gotten around to reading these particular logs yet—he is very busy with his many important duties.

APHRA:

Yeah, so important . . . giving the same lecture over and over again . . .

SANA STARROS:

And properly disciplining students. When they cause too many . . . *disruptions.*

APHRA:

[grudging]

Um, right. Good on ya, Sava Toob-Nix.

SAVA TOOB-NIX:

Well. I suppose we've wasted enough time on this digression for today. Ms. Aphra, please take your seat. Ms. Starros, thank you for bringing this new bit of scholarly research to my attention. I will have to study it on my next break from classes.

Now. Let's continue our journey into the exciting world of preservation techniques . . .

APHRA (narration):

I took my seat with as much dignity as I could muster, trying to smooth my rumpled clothes. As Sava Toob-Nix continued to drone on and on, I felt a prickle up the back of my neck. I turned ever so slightly and saw Sana Starros staring at me with those deep, dark eyes. Her gaze was so intense, so unwavering . . . it was like she was looking directly into my soul.

I might have blushed.

Ugh, recording—flag that bit for later deletion.

Even though I'd—we'd—totally humiliated Sava Toob-Nix in his classroom, I was still fully expecting him to pursue my expulsion. But he didn't. And I didn't even have to blackmail him! At least not that time.

I'm still not sure why he didn't, though—he probably could have convinced the other higher-ups at the university that Chelli Lona Aphra and her undeniable lust for unsanctioned expeditions, general impertinence, and perpetual lateness needed to be tossed out on her backside.

Hmm. I just realized this isn't really a story about me being stealthy—it's about me *trying* to be stealthy, causing a huge ruckus, and using my wits and charm to get out of it.

But that was also a skill that was going to serve the Dark Lord—in ways neither he nor I ever expected.

SCENE 7. EXT. GEONOSIS. DAY.

APHRA (narration):
Geonosis. Home of desert, droid carcasses, and . . . not much else. It's so dry, so barren, so *empty*. Even the dust clouds must get bored.

When we touched down on the surface, I was immediately re-minded of the planet my mother carted me off to in order to ensure the most dull of childhoods—like the armpit of the galaxy.

In Geonosis's case, this sheer desolation was mostly due to the entire planet being sterilized at some point.

That said, I don't think it was exactly a paradise before, either.

At least I wasn't journeying to this wasteland alone. Can you believe that at one point in her oh-so-colorful life, Chelli Lona Aphra had a whole *crew*? Despite my disarming friendliness and overwhelming natural charisma, I've never been described as a "people person." Whenever I get "people"—like those fellow students I inadvertently pitted against each other when I romanced them simultaneously—it usually ends in yelling and tragedy. And sure, my "crew," as it were, consisted of a murderous boss who did *not* like it when I questioned him or talked too much, and a pair of droids with enough firepower to blow the entire planet apart.

But still. A crew! This was a pretty major accomplishment. Teaming up with Vader was already way better than any gig I'd ever had—or at least I was determined to make it that way.

The Dark Lord was tough to read—so many long, broody silences! So much staring off into space in that dead-eyed helmet! But I'd crack him eventually. I'd already sensed he had a bit of a . . . reaction to Geonosis. His broody silences were a bit longer, his staring a bit more intense. I filed those tidbits away for later—I knew they'd come in useful. I just wasn't sure how yet.

And as soon as we landed and walked out into the dry, barren, boring-as-dust atmosphere, I did my best to give my new boss the benefit of my expertise so he could accomplish . . . uh, whatever it was he meant to accomplish.

Atmosphere: Dry winds blowing through a desolate, dusty planet. It feels as if we are surrounded by the specter of death.

APHRA:
All right, Lord Vader, here's the situation, and I promise not to skimp on the details—

DARTH VADER:
You may "skimp" if it saves valuable *time,* Aphra.

APHRA:
Yeah, a just-the-facts man. I like that. The Droid Gotra heard about a surviving Geonosian queen with a droid factory. They wanted me to liberate it from the evil carbon-based oppression.

TRIPLE-ZERO:
Oh, Mistress Aphra, I didn't realize we were about to become freedom fighters! I would have dressed up a bit—

APHRA:

You don't wear clothes—

TRIPLE-ZERO:

You'd be surprised what a simple, spanking-new plating job can do, mistress!

APHRA:

Anywaaaaaay, my plan was more along the lines of: We can steal this droid factory for us, eh?

Vader breathes, contemplating.

APHRA:

It should be quieter 'round these parts since the planet was sterilized. No queens, no hives . . . Wonder what weapon they used, would be nice to get ahold of that . . . Sorry, sorry, I'll save my fantasizing for later.

Triple-Zero, Beetee: Get going, guys. What we're after should be down through that big old cave over there—perhaps the only remotely interesting landmark on this entire planet.

TRIPLE-ZERO:

If you think it's best to send us alone, Mistress Aphra, beneath the surface of a distinctly ominous planet, certainly!

Triple-Zero and Beetee enter the cave that leads underground.

APHRA:

I sense sarcasm. Who knew droids could do sarcasm?

Ever been to Geonosis, Lord Vader?

A long, weighted beat of Vader's breathing.

DARTH VADER:

Cease your probing.

APHRA:

I'm a rogue archaeologist. You have to expect a little digging.

DARTH VADER:

I expect nothing but compliance. And *silence.* Let us follow the droids into the cave—are you certain they are capable of mapping the route?

APHRA:

Yeah, it's a tangle. But they'll be fine. Don't worry about Triple-Zero and Beetee.

DARTH VADER:

I'm not concerned about two droids. They're expendable. I come for an *army.*

Aphra and Darth Vader follow Triple-Zero and Beetee into the cave.

Atmosphere: This is like a haunted house—the only sign of life on the planet, but incredibly creepy. Weird echoes, ominous clanks. You really feel that something bad is around every corner.

APHRA (narration):

As we descended into the cave, I probably should have been feeling at least the teeniest, tiniest drop of . . . *unease.* I mean, as thrillingly daring as my adventures often are, I don't think I've ever blithely walked into a creepy subterranean lair that possibly houses a secret droid factory with a disgraced Sith Lord.

But honestly, the fact that it was a serious level up from anything I'd ever done? *That's* what made it so exciting. Despite his threats, I could tell Vader saw my potential: Unlike Sava Toob-Nix, he was all about the unsanctioned, unapproved, totally off-the-grid expedition. And even if he didn't show it, I knew he was impressed that I'd had the out-of-the-box brainstorm to bring him here. He appreciated my *initiative.*

Of course, this mission was also totally dangerous—possibly more dangerous than anything I'd attempted before. But hey—that didn't really bother me. I just kept thinking: If I died right this moment, what would they say about me?

Doctor Aphra: rogue archaeologist who had tons of swashbuckling, death-defying adventures finally slain on a top-secret mission with Darth Vader!

Er. I guess since it was top secret maybe they wouldn't say that part, but the point is: I'd be fine with that existing as the final word on my life. I'd have no regrets.

Hopefully, though, I'd live long enough to make this extremely intriguing situation work for me.

So I kept following Vader into the winding caverns.

True to their word, Triple-Zero and Beetee forged ahead and made a terrifying discovery: a whole gang of angry battle droids! Gigantic and clanking, these droids' joints clearly hadn't been oiled for millennia. Their metal bits were battle-damaged and riddled with holes—but their piercing eyes glowed vibrant red, even in the dark of the cave. And they'd clearly been . . . altered in some ways. They had massive metal wings unfurling from their backs, the clicks and clanks echoing through the dark.

It made them look like monsters from the stories my mother had told me when I was young: soul-stealing goblins who like to eat cute little kids for breakfast.

Triple-Zero greeted them in his usual friendly manner.

TRIPLE-ZERO:
Hello, sirs. I presume you speak Geonosian Hive-Mind? A language I am more than fluent in!

Alas, I have nothing to say. Beetee, if you will . . .

Beetee unleashes a wall of fiery explosions.

APHRA (narration):
And Beetee . . . *also* greeted them in *his* usual friendly manner!

By the end of his little "hello," the winged battle droids were lying everywhere in pieces. And most of those pieces were on fire.

TRIPLE-ZERO:
Thank you, Beetee!

Sirs, now that I've had a moment to think about it, a few words *do* spring to mind, which I will relay in Geonosian Hive-Mind so that you fully understand . . .

[a line of Geonosian here that translates to . . .]

APHRA (narration):
I believe that translates roughly to: "Hahaha! You are on fire and also dead!"

Once Vader and I got to the scene, *everything* was pretty much on fire, but as I knelt down to survey the wreckage, I could still make out the remnants of droidlike components. And as we ventured deeper into the cave—to the queen's subterranean lair—I couldn't help but hypothesize out loud. Even if Lord Vader occasionally seemed annoyed by my chitter-chatter, I knew he appreciated the kind of brilliant theorizing that had led us here. And I had plenty more where that came from. What can I say? This girl loves a hypothesis.

Aphra, Vader, Triple-Zero, and Beetee continue their descent into the depths of the cave.

APHRA:
So the Gotra's leads are on the money. There *is* an active factory down here. Interesting tweaks on the standard droid design, too—the wings and all. I suspect the queen doesn't see these as droids.

I suppose that makes sense. Immortal queen, sterilized. The urge to continue the species by any means necessary. So when biology fails, she turns to science.

They aren't droids to her . . . they're *children.*

APHRA (narration):
We turned that last corner, and . . . boy howdy, I'm not even sure how to describe what we saw.

I mean, it was the queen. Obviously.

GEONOSIAN QUEEN:
Hissssss . . .

APHRA (narration):
I've encountered a lot of fearsome-looking creatures in my time. She wasn't the biggest, she wasn't the ugliest . . . but something about the way her sharp black eyes bored into us with such hatred, her mouthful of long, sharp teeth bared, each of her eight . . . arms? Legs? *Appendages* twitching, ready to tear us apart . . . and that regal half-moon that crowned the top of her head swaying violently . . .

[shudder]

Wait, what was I saying?

Oh, right.

She was absolutely *terrifying*.

She was positioned in her chamber, a pit where she had managed to permanently attach herself to the twisting metal and maze of wires that was the droid factory, and was surrounded by her hive . . . womb . . . whatever you want to call it. Slime-encrusted glowing orbs formed a wall behind her. These were her children. And she was going to protect them by any means necessary.

Being a seasoned expert in all manner of terrifying things, I kept my cool.

Even when one of her slime-encrusted robot egg things *hatched*.

One of the queen's eggs hatches open, revealing yet another murderous, winged battle droid.

APHRA:
And now for our devilishly clever plan to steal a robot womb factory from a homicidally broody alien queen. Do you still think this is a good idea, Lord Vader?

DARTH VADER:
Yes.

APHRA (narration):
I'll be honest—there was a moment where I wasn't sure what his answer was going to be. It could've gone either way.

Again, this is what made things exciting.

But half a second later, there he went, drawing his lightsaber and launching himself at said homicidally broody alien queen in what I would describe as a decidedly aggressive manner.

Vader launches himself at the Geonosian queen, drawing his lightsaber.

GEONOSIAN QUEEN:
You! Why are you here? Has the Emperor not taken enough from the Geonosians with your bombs?

DARTH VADER:
No.

APHRA (narration):
Oh man. Of course the Empire had something to do with this planet dying—maybe that's why Vader'd had such a . . . reaction to the place. But *this* was the kind of Darth Vader action I'd been hoping for. He sliced through the air with his lightsaber, severing her connection to the factory she'd been using as a womb.

And then the Dark Lord and the Geonosian queen faced off against each other, his hand raised—doing one of those magical-type Force things again. The Geonosian queen may have possessed sharp teeth and have a buncha killer winged robots at her disposal, but she definitely did *not* have magical-type Force things! How was she possibly going to respond?

GEONOSIAN QUEEN:
Stop them! They've ruined our past—they can't destroy our future!

Children—stop him!

A battalion of winged battle droids descends, surrounding Vader.

APHRA (narration):
Oh. That's how. Call upon your army of winged battle droids, always does the trick.

But let's not forget, Vader and I had our own army . . . of two.

APHRA:
Triple-Zero, Beetee: Now!

Beetee lets loose with another fiery blast, directly into the queen's chamber.

APHRA:
Good job, boys. You know, some people have asked me: Why would a droid need a flamethrower? I always say . . . Why not?

Now deploying the location beacon to . . . *oh no.*

APHRA (narration):
We had a problem. So I did what *any* top-tier adventurer would do . . . I jumped into the queen's chamber.

Yes, into the pit filled with fire, exploding mutant droids, and one determined Dark Lord facing off against an increasingly furious alien about to be robbed of her precious brood.

What could go wrong?

APHRA:
Lord Vader!

I can't get the location beacon to the roof. The thrusters have gone. Can you . . .

APHRA (narration):
I didn't even have to complete that sentence. Lord Vader used yet another Force thing—and with the simple lift of a finger, he sent the location beacon careening all the way up to the roof of the queen's lair.

APHRA:

Of course you can. You're Darth Vader. And now I can call my ship.

Aphra to *Ark Angel.* Barrage to location—now!

The Ark Angel *fires on the queen's chamber, causing the whole lair to cave in—rocks crash to the floor. Vader uses Force energy to protect himself and Aphra from the avalanche.*

APHRA (narration):

It was . . . wow. Rocks falling everywhere. Vader throwing a hand up, summoning an invisible field of Force energy to surround us. I'd like to say I was right there, fighting alongside him . . . somehow.

But I actually threw myself to the ground, arms flying up instinctively to protect my head.

And through it all, I could still hear the screams of the Geonosian queen . . .

GEONOSIAN QUEEN:

My womb! My children! Bring me back my children!

APHRA (narration):

As her empire crumbled around her, Vader's ship swooped through the now exposed Geonosian sky above us—no, not the TIE fighter, his *other* ship, you think Darth Vader only has one ship? We knew this mission would require *multiple* ships, and luckily the Dark Lord still possessed a few of the luxuries Dark Lords enjoy.

Vader's ship lowered an electromagnetic crane through the newly formed hole in the cave's ceiling. I attached the crane to the womb-slash-droid-factory, and we all hopped on board.

I spared a glance at the graceful, elegant lines of Vader's ship above us—so shiny, so regal . . .

APHRA:

Are you sure your ship can lift this? The *Ark Angel* is a heavy-duty lifter. Yours looks like a pretty little thing, but—

DARTH VADER:
Do not worry. She's stronger than she looks.

APHRA (narration):
The queen never stopped screaming. Not even as we were lifted to the sky.

GEONOSIAN QUEEN:
My empire is forever! My empire cannot end!

APHRA (narration):
Sometimes I can still hear her screaming. Sometimes I think maybe I was screaming, too.

But . . . whatever. We did it! My first successful mission with the one and only Darth Vader. My first step in gaining his trust . . . so I could use it to my advantage later.

What a triumph, right?

As we soared over the crumbling ruins of the queen's lair, towed by Vader's ship to safety, I looked out once more at the desolate landscape. I thought maybe the fact that I'd just led a high-stakes droid factory heist that culminated with a lot of stuff blowing up would change my feelings toward the place. Maybe it would now appear more . . . exciting?

But, nah. Same old desert. Same old boring.

We were taking the most exciting parts with us.

SCENE 8. INT. THE *ARK ANGEL*. LATER.

APHRA (narration):
Back on the *Ark Angel,* I used the incredible mechanical expertise—
you know, the expertise Vader had taken special note of—to power
up our brand-spankin'-new droid factory. The factory spoke to me
in that secret language—it told me it was just ever so grateful to be
part of our sure-to-be-galaxy-shattering mission. And, like
magic—or the Force, I guess?—it started spitting out perfectly
formed commando 'bots.

With a clank and a whoosh, a droid slides out of the droid factory.

APHRA (narration):
Well . . . perfect according to *me,* anyway.

TRIPLE-ZERO:
Hmm. *Not* perfect. Teething issues. Nothing that can't be fixed.
Perhaps I should try generating some of the terribly interesting
wings we saw on the queen's droids? And we could always try *my*
favorite enhancement methods, masters!

DARTH VADER:

What does the droid wish to do?

APHRA:

It's a long story. Triple-Zero has some unconventional theories about self-improvement for droids—

TRIPLE-ZERO:

I think you mean liberation, Mistress Aphra! And liberating these droids is the least you can do, considering that you've stolen them away from the only home they've ever known.

APHRA:

Awww, Trip. Didn't think you were such a softie.

TRIPLE-ZERO:

I contain a multitude of unprobed depths, as you organics would say.

APHRA:

Is . . . that what we would say?

TRIPLE-ZERO:

Or something equally pithy and meaningless, mistress.

DARTH VADER:

As you were saying, Doctor—the droid has ideas?

APHRA:

Mmm, yeah, probably nothing we actually want to try, your lordliness, unless you want to end up a fleshy smear on the ship's floor. It's the main reason Trip's consciousness was locked away.

DARTH VADER:

I see . . .

APHRA:

But in a few hours, you'll have your droid army. Some minor tweaks to get it 100 percent, but nothing Beetee can't handle.

BEETEE:

BLEEP!

APHRA:

So . . . my lord. I have a question for you.

A weighted beat of Vader's breathing.

APHRA:

Are you planning on killing me now or later?

A weighted beat of Vader's breathing.

APHRA:

You have a private off-the-grid army for whatever you're planning next. You don't need me anymore. I knew my clock was ticking the second you stepped off your TIE fighter.

If I get a choice, I'd like the lightsaber right through the neck. No warning. Nice and quick.

If I get a veto, ejection into space. Always had nightmares about that. Brrr.

A weighted beat of Vader's breathing.

APHRA:

I act glib, but I'm not stupid. The way I've lived, I know I'm lucky to be alive.

I'd rather not die, you understand. But I'm happy my blood's doodling in the margins of a story worth telling.

A weighted beat of Vader's breathing.

DARTH VADER:

You have proved yourself resourceful. You are safe for as long as I have use of you.

If you try to blackmail me, you will find your plans confounded and your life at an end.

APHRA:

You know, you *can* trust me. But you shouldn't. I am a walking, talking, stupid risk. You need to *win,* Lord Vader. This is for a higher cause.

When you need to do it, *do it*.

And lightsaber, please.

TRIPLE-ZERO:
I'm sorry to interrupt, masters! I have a signal from a bounty hunter.

DARTH VADER:
Fett? Has he found the boy?

APHRA:
Boy . . . ?

DARTH VADER:
Now is not the time, Aphra.

APHRA:
But—

DARTH VADER:
Not the time.

TRIPLE-ZERO:
Not Fett, sir. It's one Krrsantan, Black.

DARTH VADER:
The Wookiee?

TRIPLE-ZERO:
He claims to have a very important delivery for you!

APHRA (narration):
Trust Triple-Zero to totally interrupt a touching bonding moment between me and my new boss.

The "important delivery" ended up being some poor soul the fearsome Wookiee bounty hunter Black Krrsantan had captured. And he was about to bring this unlucky organic aboard for Triple-Zero to torture information out of—I guess that's why Trip sounded so excited.

TRIPLE-ZERO:
Oh, this will be just *glorious*. If I believed in the Maker, I would thank them for allowing Black Krrsantan to bring me such a won-

derful gift. My first organic torture since my reawakening. It's been ever so long, but you know what they say: You never forget just how soft human flesh is, how *pliant* . . . especially when needles are involved!

DARTH VADER:
Do whatever you must.

APHRA (narration):
I must admit, I was struck by the note of . . . eagerness that flitted into Vader's voice when he asked if the bounty hunter Boba Fett had found "the boy." True, it might not have sounded like "eagerness" on anyone else—it was a wisp, a hint, the slightest alteration in vocal cadence. And because I was starting to truly know him, I could hear it.

Who was this "boy," and what boy could ever be that important to Darth Vader? I *needed* to find out.

But part of maneuvering around Darth Vader means knowing when to shut up—so that's what I did. For now.

I was also still stuck on the Dark Lord's eventual plan for my death.

I studied his mask as he listened to Triple-Zero's excited blatherings . . .

TRIPLE-ZERO:
[slight in background, not interrupting speech]

—and *that's* when I usually deploy my other neurotoxin, the one I only use for special occasions! Then again, it's always a special occasion when I get to drain an organic of its lifeblood!

APHRA (narration):
Had Vader heard me? Did he understand? Had I disgusted him with my plea, even though it had been delivered in an offhand, carefree kind of way?

While I was learning to read him better . . . with this, I was getting *nothing*.

That mask, that *shield* against Darth Vader's countenance, is legendary. And I can confirm: It is about a billion percent more intimidating up close. Something about those glassy black pits where his eyes should be . . . when you stare into them, they really do look like the Void. Endless black . . . and only the occasional blurry reflection of your timid face staring back at you. The longer I stared into his eyes, all I saw were *mine,* desperate to know how he planned on killing me.

I mean. To the outside observer, I don't think I looked desperate. I've *learned* how not to look desperate. How not to be *weak.*

But since I know myself exceptionally well, *I* could see it.

Anyway, the whole lightsaber thing . . . if this exciting life of mine was going to end . . . I know it might sound like I was choosing efficiency over epicness. And normally I'd choose *the most epic thing* every time.

But whenever I imagined being ejected into space, the cold and the dark . . . the sheer terror of confronting this big old universe without the comforting hum of a ship around me, that mechanical language whispering my name . . .

I knew I'd be scared in a way I'd never been scared before. And I couldn't have that. I couldn't be *weak* that way.

Weakness—as you know better than anyone—is the one thing I can never show. Even to the Void. I think that's why I've gotten so good at finding it in others.

A lightsaber through the neck wouldn't give me time to be weak. It would just happen.

Choppity-chop, we're done.

But . . . I was also kind of hoping, even at this early stage of our partnership, that Vader had already seen how valuable I could be. That I'd started to prove the potential he'd sensed in me existed, and I was ready to surpass his expectations—really blow 'em out of the water.

I turned away from his mask, from my reflection—from my desperate eyes, trying so hard to believe, just this once . . . that I'd found something real. Something that would give me everything I wanted. If only I could crack his armor and break through—without breaking myself.

SCENE 9. INT. UNIVERSITY OF BAR'LETH LIBRARY. DAY. FLASHBACK.

APHRA (narration):
Anywaaaaaay . . . sorry, why am I getting all angsty? That is *so* not me.

Triple-Zero got what he needed out of Vader's new prisoner, the location of some sort of secret research base, which ended up being our next destination. The Dark Lord boarded this big ol' bad-guy ship with his newly generated droid army to . . . well, to be honest, I'm not actually sure what all he was up to, but I guess it involved Emperor Palpatine training a bunch of losers who were meant to be Vader's successors.

As someone who was currently sucking up all the Vader-related info I could so I'd know how to best manipulate him, I could've told ol' Palpy this was a bad idea.

And I really wanted to tell the Dark Lord I understood what he was going through. Like I said before, no one in my life has ever really seen me—and the beautiful rainbow of skills I'm capable of. I suppose some would argue that I'm always moving too fast and too, uh, tornado-like? For them to *be able* to see me.

But how could the Emperor not see Darth Vader? Sure, he'd screwed up a little with the Death Star business. He was still one of the most purely powerful people in the galaxy—I'd been able to see that immediately.

But . . . perhaps he also moved too fast. Perhaps his mind was always whirling with possibilities he couldn't quiet or calm. Perhaps he never thought ahead to the potential consequences for his death-defying actions.

Yes, I know. Now you're thinking: *Way to project, Chelli! Aren't you really talking about yourself?*

Maybe. But that was just another sign that I was *connecting* with the Dark Lord.

I've also come to believe that if you have to slow down in order for someone to see you . . . well, maybe it's not worth it. Take me and Sana. After the incident with Sava Toob-Nix, I ran into her again at the campus library. She was sitting at one of the library's long tables, studying—she was *always* studying back in those days, her hair falling over her face like the most regal of waterfalls.

I had to resist the urge to brush it out of the way so I could see those dark eyes, that perfectly furrowed brow—

Ugh. Getting mushy, Aphra.

Recording: Mark this spot to edit later, I need to clean up some of my more flowery language.

Anyway, *I* wasn't at the library to study—I was trying to stealthily return a particularly rare text that was never meant to be checked out. (Frankly: kind of a shortsighted rule since these kinds of texts were all like a thousand pages, and it simply wasn't possible to look through them in the miserly one-hour slot the library allotted for rare-book viewing.)

I was skulking my way up the stairs to the library's top level when I heard that whiskey shot of a voice ring out—

SANA STARROS:
Aphra?

APHRA:
Agghhhhhh!

APHRA (narration):
Yeah, I reacted super gracefully, letting out a yelp that reverberated through the entire library and dropping that super-rare text with such an alarming thunk, I cringed.

I cringed even more when it clunked its way down the stairs.

We hear the book thunk-thunk-thunk down the stairs.

APHRA (narration):
Oof. I plastered on a huge, cheesy grin and tiptoed back down the stairs, toward the fallen book soldier.

Not that it made any difference—everyone was still staring at me. Especially *her.*

Sana rushed to my side as I knelt to pick up the book—which had definitely gotten a little . . . dog-eared.

SANA STARROS:
Sorry, sorry. I just . . . saw you. And it looked like you had the *Tome of Ancient Crait* with you . . . but isn't that one of the rare texts we're not supposed to remove from the library?

APHRA:
Um, maybe. I guess. Yes. Hence my skulking.

SANA STARROS:
That was skulking?

APHRA:
I was being all stealthy-like.

SANA STARROS:
I don't think *you* could ever be stealthy-like.

APHRA:
Um, excuse you—I'm totally good at stealth—

SANA STARROS:
Oh, I see. Yeah, that time you tried to sneak into a lecture through a window and almost made Sava Toob-Nix's head explode—that was definitely stealthy.

APHRA:
He had it coming.

SANA STARROS:
No argument there.

APHRA (narration):
We sorta . . . I guess you could say . . . smiled at each other, then.

Ughhhhh. Recording, mark this spot for editing, too!

Sana took the book from me, our fingertips brushing. And a little bit of indescribable electricity ran up my arm.

SANA STARROS:
Wow. Look at these hand-drawn depictions of the ancient artifacts in the cave dwellings—I've been dying to study these in more detail. But the time limit, it's so . . . so . . .

APHRA:
Limiting. I know.

APHRA (narration):
I watched her for a moment as she ran her fingertips over the book's beautiful watercolor illustrations, her eyes lighting up with the soft glow of curiosity and inspiration. Like she was discovering the key to the history of the world.

I know, I'm being flowery again. I'm just trying to . . . *explain* why I did what I did next.

APHRA:

[sotto]

Hey. Let's get out of here.

SANA STARROS:

But . . . you have to put the book back! Isn't that what you were about to do—

APHRA:

I changed my mind. Let's take it with us.

SANA STARROS:

But . . . but . . . we made such a ruckus, and the front-desk librarian is heading this way . . .

OFFICIOUS LIBRARIAN:

Ladies! May I help you with something?

APHRA:

Exactly. So let's go. *Now.*

OFFICIOUS LIBRARIAN:

Is that Chelli Lona Aphra? Young lady, I've been meaning to talk to you—

APHRA:

Come on. She doesn't know we have the book!

OFFICIOUS LIBRARIAN:

I know it was you who took that rare book!

APHRA:

. . . oh. Come *on*!

APHRA (narration):

I grabbed her hand and we booked it outta there, the precious tome shoved unceremoniously under my shirt. Right as we reached the exit—and right as that cranky old librarian nearly reached *us*—I pulled the book out and tossed it to Sana.

APHRA:

Here, catch! And split up!

APHRA (narration):

I went one way, she went the other. I still remember her face—her cheeks flushed, her eyes sparkling with the thrill of getting away with something so illicit. I don't think I'd ever seen Sana Starros looking like she was having so much *fun.*

It would have been better if we'd left it that way—that simple, pure moment of joy, frozen in time.

Or . . . actually, it would have been *best* if I'd taken off before she'd even come up to me. Refused to slow down. Never spoken to her. Just left things with me attracting her notice after interrupting Sava Toob-Nix's lecture.

Instead we had to go and mess everything up.

If only we'd never seen each other again.

SCENE 10. INT. VADER'S SHIP.

APHRA (narration):
Vader was tied up at the bad-guy research facility for a while. Trip and Beetee had gone with him, so that left me all by my lonesome on Vader's ship—the sleek, shiny one that lifted us out of the Geonosian queen's lair.

At first this was cool.

Then it got boring.

The Dark Lord had specifically instructed me to only contact him if there was an emergency.

He also told me not to touch anything.

Buuuuut . . . I figured as long as I left things *basically* the way I found them, what was the harm?

APHRA:
Hmm, I've eaten all the food in the galley; slid down the hall in my socks; tested, taken apart, and reassembled every weapon in the

armory . . . what now, what now . . . ooh, I wonder what this big, red button does?

BOBA FETT (on comm):
Vader, do you copy? It's Fett. I'm on an encrypted channel—the Imps won't hear us.

APHRA:
Um, hello! Yes! *Copy that!* Lord Vader is . . . indisposed at the moment, but this is his most trusted attaché!

BOBA FETT (on comm):
I've heard *nothing* about an attaché.

APHRA:
You're on an encrypted channel, and Vader asked you to make especially sure the Imperials wouldn't hear whatever it is you need to talk about. You don't think the Dark Lord has *other* secrets?

BOBA FETT (on comm):
Tell him I'm ready to report.

APHRA:
Is it about the boy?

BOBA FETT (on comm):
My report is only to be delivered to Vader—

APHRA:
I've told you: I'm Vader's most trusted attaché. I know *everything*. In fact, I know so much, it's very possible that I already know what *you* know and have already told him all about it—

BOBA FETT (on comm):
You haven't. If you had, Vader would be on the move.

APHRA:
Okay, ya got me. I may have the information, but I haven't told him anything—so you should still be good to collect your bounty—

BOBA FETT (on comm):
Not possible. I lost the boy.

APHRA:

But surely you still got some kind of *information,* or you wouldn't be making a report—you'd be running from Lord Vader as fast as your bounty-huntin' butt could carry you.

BOBA FETT (on comm):

This information is crucial enough that I *will* be collecting part of my fee . . .

APHRA:

So tell me whatcha got. And if it's something I already know, I promise not to tell Vader. If it's something I *don't* know . . . well. I can tell you if it's info he'll actually pay for. Either way, you collect the bounty and Vader lets you live. Win–win.

BOBA FETT (on comm):

Why should I trust you?

APHRA:

Oh, you definitely shouldn't! But as I see it, if you don't tell me . . . well, the reverse of either of the scenarios I just described ends with you dead, on the run, or at the very least . . . on Darth Vader's bad side.

Let me just say: We don't know each other super well, but I don't want that for you!

BOBA FETT (on comm):

Very well. But if you cross me, things will end badly for *you* as well.

APHRA:

Understood. Give up the goods, Boba Man!

BOBA FETT (on comm):

Fett. Boba *Fett.* All I have is a name. The boy's name is . . .

APHRA (narration):

Whoa, time to cue the dramatic music! This reveal was gonna be *big* . . .

Dramatic music swells . . .

BOBA FETT (on comm):
Skywalker.

The dramatic music abruptly cuts off.

APHRA:
Who?

BOBA FETT (on comm):
You . . . said you knew this already . . .

APHRA:
Yeah, yeah, I do . . . I mean. I think I do. I might have been thinking of some *other* boy, remind me why Vader's so hot for this one, again?

BOBA FETT (on comm):
I will wait until I can speak to Darth Vader myself . . .

APHRA:
Please! Otherwise I won't pass on your message at all, I'll erase any evidence you ever contacted the ship, and I'll tell my lord that Boba Fett is spreading rumors all over the galaxy that Darth Vader is a big *scaredy-cat* who—

BOBA FETT (on comm):
He's the boy who destroyed the Death Star.

APHRA (narration):
A-ha! Now I was really getting somewhere. Grabbing on to every new tidbit of information. Every *opportunity.*

Of course, I wasn't entirely sure what all this meant yet. My best strategy for now was to go ahead and do what I'd promised—invite Boba Man on board our ship and let him deliver the information to Vader himself. I already knew Vader well enough to know he wouldn't . . . appreciate *this* kind of initiative, me weaseling out info he clearly wanted to keep private.

But it would be useful to me later, I could feel it. Maybe Vader would even come to trust me enough that he'd confide in me himself.

So. Vader was after the boy who destroyed the Death Star. I suppose that made sense. I mean, what the hell, you work for years on all of your Force magic stuff, you ascend the ranks to become the ultimate Dark Lord of the galaxy, and then some rebel pilot asshole swoops in and blows up your greatest achievement yet. I'd be upset, too!

As I pondered that further, I realized Vader had actually been gone for a while. I tried contacting him, no dice.

So I gathered all those weapons I'd just lovingly tested out and prepared to mount a rescue mission . . . only to have the Dark Lord return in a huff.

APHRA:
What happened? I was tooling up to come in after you and—

DARTH VADER:
Silence.

APHRA:
Lord Vader, I—

DARTH VADER:
This would not be a good time to bait me, Aphra.

APHRA:
I know. I have a message from the other bounty hunter. Boba Fett. He caught up with . . . with that boy you're so interested in. He wants to report.

DARTH VADER:
I will see him.

APHRA:
Good, he's standing by, waiting to board. He'll meet you in your, uh . . . throne room? Control center? Place on the ship where really cool stuff happens? Whatever you call it . . .

APHRA (narration):
As Vader left for his meeting with Fett, I gazed out into the vast starscape, those endless pinpricks of light against velvety darkness.

I felt the hum of the ship in my bones, that secret language speaking to me. I settled in and smiled to myself, thinking of all the delicious information I'd already been able to gather.

Where would we go next?

I had no idea.

Excitement skittered up my spine.

And I thought: *This is the greatest job of my life.*

SCENE 11. INT. APHRA'S FAMILY HOME. SECOND MOON OF THRINITTIK. NIGHT. FLASHBACK.

APHRA (narration):
What charming locales was my new job about to take me to? I kept picturing a jaunt through the breathtaking clouds of Yama'chen. An underwater excursion to the bluest lakes of Naboo.

I know you're probably scoffing at me wishing for my death-defying capers to take place in picturesque locales.

"What do you really want, Chelli?" you might say. "An adventure or a vacation?"

First of all, I don't believe in making such choices. Why not both?

Second, can you blame me for wanting an aesthetically pleasing excursion?

A lot of my "almost died" life experiences happened on the most desolate, barren, flat-out boring planets. If I'm already dying, at least give me something nice to look at.

The very first time I almost died was on the most backwater of burgs: Arbiflux, a forest world in the *outer* Outer Rim, which is where my mother took me after she and my dad split up when I was just a kid.

Or perhaps more accurately: after she decided she could no longer live with my father's obsessive quest for Jedi artifacts and his need to achieve *greatness*—even if it put us in harm's way.

I can still hear them arguing, me creeping up to the edge of my dad's workshop when I was supposed to be asleep in my bed . . .

KORIN APHRA:

It's only a three-day trip, Lona! We won't even leave the system, I just need some records from the university library on the fifth moon—

LONA APHRA:

I understand that part, Korin—well, I *mostly* understand it, even though there are perfectly good libraries here. I thought that's why we moved to the University Quarter—

KORIN APHRA:

I've received several unverified reports that *this* library has secret records documenting the Knights of the Ordu Aspectu—if they exist, I need to get to them before the Imperials have them destroyed—

LONA APHRA:

"Unverified reports" . . . "*If* they exist" . . . do you hear yourself? You're willing to put us in the line of an Imperial firing squad—or *worse*—for unsubstantiated hunches and flights of fancy. And you want to take our child with you!

APHRA (narration):

Look, my dad is *not* in the running for any Parent of the Millennium awards. Or even Parent of the Last Fifteen Minutes. But if I'm choosing, I'll always choose "potential harm's way" over "safe but so mind-numbingly dull that you spend most days counting dust motes on the crumbling leaves of chatterplants." At least Dad had a purpose in life. Mom's purpose was mostly "don't die."

KORIN APHRA:
Chelli is interested in my research—

LONA APHRA:
Chelli is *six*!

KORIN APHRA:
And already, she shows such promise—I could really use her help on this trip. She's so fascinated by my work—whenever I talk about how restoring the Knights could bring light and balance to the galaxy . . . I can see that yearning in her eyes. That desire to make her mark, to change the world, to be great.

She *wants* to do incredible things in her life, Lona. She's like me: never satisfied with simply existing. She wants to *live*.

LONA APHRA:
Then why do you want to take her on a dangerous research trip where she'll probably end up dead?

YOUNG APHRA:
Mama! Daddy!

APHRA (narration):
Yes, this is where I decided—strategically—to emerge. I wasn't the smartest kid, but I knew that as soon as I toddled in, looking all cute and helpless, they'd pay attention to me and stop fighting.

Hmm, you know what? Actually, I *was* pretty smart.

YOUNG APHRA:
Why are you yelling?

LONA APHRA:
Oh, Chelli . . . we're just having a . . . discussion . . .

KORIN APHRA:
That's right, Little Boop! Say . . . how would you like to go on a super-important research mission with your dad—

LONA APHRA:
Korin!

[sotto, gritted teeth]

We're not finished talking about this. And we never agreed—

KORIN APHRA:
No, we can't agree. So it should be up to Chelli, don't you think? She's perfectly capable of making her own decisions—

LONA APHRA:
She's *a child*—

KORIN APHRA:
Nonsense. You're a big girl, aren't you, Little Boop?

YOUNG APHRA:
Um . . . yeah?

KORIN APHRA:
So what do *you* want to do? Stay here and play with your tooka? Or go on an adventure with your dad?

YOUNG APHRA:
Adventure!

KORIN APHRA:
Then adventure it shall be!

LONA APHRA:
Korin . . .

KORIN APHRA:
She's decided, Lona—she wants to expand her horizons. And that's that.

APHRA (narration):
I did go on that mission with my dad, despite my mom's protests. And actually, for all my parents' arguing . . . nothing really happened. My dad got the records he was after, and the only dangerous part was he had to bribe one of the librarians to get what he

wanted—and to let us leave with stuff we weren't supposed to even touch in the first place.

But still. It was definitely the most exciting thing that had happened to me in my young life. Even at six, I didn't have any trepidation about going. The danger of the unknown called to me— I craved that anticipatory thrill skittering up my spine more than I craved anything.

Okay, okay . . . I also wanted my dad to pay attention to me. And the only time he did that was when I was pretending to be interested in his Jedi doohickey research.

Of course . . . as I learned on that trip, the *real* reason he wanted me to go . . . well, it wasn't because he sensed greatness in a six-year-old. It was because I was small enough to slip into hidden nooks and crannies, cute enough to distract the librarians when my dad was trying to pull stuff out of said nooks and crannies . . . and I had extra hands to help him carry the stuff he wanted offworld.

KORIN APHRA:
[like an echo of the past]

Well done, Little Boop! Now make sure you don't drop that scroll, it's *very* valuable.

APHRA (narration):
Really, my dad could have taken *any* small child with him on this trip. Didn't have to be me. I was useful, but not essential.

Buuuuuut . . . I'm pretty sure my dad carting his impressionable daughter to that crumbling library on the Fifth Moon of Thrinittik was the last straw for my mom—one in a very long series of straws.

I know there were smaller moments after that that factored in . . . but I think *that's* when she decided.

And that's how the great Chelli Lona Aphra ended up on the forest world of Arbiflux, counting dust motes on chatterplants.

SCENE 12. EXT. APHRA'S FAMILY HOMESTEAD. ARBIFLUX. THE *OUTER* OUTER RIM. DAY. FLASHBACK.

Atmosphere: There is a barren dullness to this world, but it has more of a wild frontier feeling than, say, Tatooine or Geonosis. Weird creatures are lurking around corners, wildlife is trying to break through the drought, and we should get a sense of a world not yet tamed. Perhaps we hear constant chitterings from the chatter-plants as well—like crickets.

APHRA (narration):
The words *forest world* really paint a picture. Lush, verdant greenery. Interesting beasties around every corner. Tangled woods, made for exploring.

That is . . . *not* what Arbiflux was.

I guess there was a drought happening around that time in the *outer* Outer Rim, because the trees all around our humble homestead were withered and dying, their branches turning to dust. The grass was so dry, it crunched underneath your feet. And the air was murky and thick, pressing down on you from the moment you woke up to yet another excruciatingly dull morning.

YOUNG APHRA:
Why did you bring me here? I *hate* it.

LONA APHRA:
It's home now, Little Boop. You'll learn to love it. And we'll be safe here.

APHRA (narration):
Hmph. How did my mother not know me at all? That just made me hate it *more*.

And for the record: She was wrong. It was not *safe*. Remember the "almost dying" thing?

It happened on a day like any other—because every day on Arbiflux was exactly the same. I was minding my own business, counting all those amazing dust motes . . . when raiders came.

LONA APHRA:
No!

As Lona screams, we hear the sounds of blasterfire.

YOUNG APHRA:
Mom . . . ?

APHRA (narration):
I remember the sounds of blasterfire. The chatterplants screeching, trying to warn us.

I remember my mother's arm being shot clean off.

LONA APHRA:
Chelli . . . *run!*

YOUNG APHRA:
But . . . Mama . . .

LONA APHRA:
Now! I'll . . . I'll be right behind you . . . take my blaster . . .

APHRA (narration):
I also remember that for one small, shameful moment . . . my primary emotion wasn't fear.

It was . . . excitement. Yes, that same excitement I felt when I leapt into the fiery pit of the homicidal Geonosian queen, when I tripped the sensor while liberating the Triple-Zero Matrix . . . when Darth Vader offered me his hand.

Because here on this most backwater of planets, this "safe" little homestead . . . something was finally *happening*.

I didn't live in that surge of excitement, though. My instincts took over and I followed Mom's advice: I ran.

Young Aphra's footfalls and heavy breathing overtake the sounds of blasterfire.

APHRA (narration):
I ran through the dried-up trees of that backward burg . . . and so far that I actually found the part of the forest that was green, lush, beautiful. If only my mother had let me explore that part. If only she hadn't been so obsessed with keeping me "safe."

She managed to follow me for part of it, stumbling behind. Yelling at me not to turn around, not to look back.

But she was losing blood so fast . . . her *arm* . . .

This is where I learned: Never look behind you.

When she finally collapsed . . . well, I did turn. I did look.

I saw her die.

And then I turned back and shot at those raiders with all my might.

YOUNG APHRA:
Get back!

Young Aphra fires on the raiders.

APHRA (narration):

Every nerve in my body was focused on fighting back, on getting them to *leave,* on hoping against hope my mom was somehow okay . . . even though I knew she wasn't. Tears streamed down my cheeks . . . and then the most extraordinary thing happened . . .

Lightning cracks through the sky, and it starts to rain. Perhaps we hear the chitterings from local wildlife getting louder as the rain gets heavier . . .

APHRA (narration):

It started to *rain.*

It was like this dust-dry, boring-ass world had suddenly decided to become . . . *interesting.*

But at that point, my excitement had faded.

Now I was just scared.

I fired and fired and fired.

At the time, I wasn't ready to die. My blood wasn't prepared to doodle the margins of history.

But that's because I hadn't really *lived* yet.

I hadn't found an epic quest worth pursuing.

When Darth Vader recruited me, I felt that click into place—just as surely as I feel it when I crack a safe or reactivate a troublesome droid. Somehow, *this* was going to be my epic quest. Vader sensed actual greatness in me, not just the ability to help cart old Jedi scrolls offworld. I still hadn't totally earned his trust, but once I did . . . well, the possibilities were endless.

And it was going to happen. I just knew it.

I couldn't wait to see where we were going next.

I was really hoping for Naboo. The *Ark Angel* would do such lovely acrobatic maneuvers over all those lakes.

Please be Naboo, please be Naboo . . .

SCENE 13. EXT. SKYWALKER HOMESTEAD. TATOOINE. DAY.

Atmosphere: Winds blowing through a barren desert. This one is perhaps less scorched than Geonosis—it feels abandoned, but more like the inhabitants are really into keeping to themselves. There is life here—but it's been frightened inside.

APHRA:

Tatooine? Are you kidding me?

DARTH VADER:

You will go where I have need of you.

APHRA:

Y-yes. Of course, my lord. It just seems like a rather, ah, unconventional choice for someone of your stature. Not much for a secret droid army to shoot at here on Tatooine.

DARTH VADER:

The boy who destroyed the Death Star has . . . connections to this place. And it was on this planet that he bested Boba Fett.

APHRA:
[sotto]

Oh reaaalllly . . . huh, Boba Man didn't tell me that part . . .

DARTH VADER:
What was that, Doctor?

APHRA:
Nothing.

DARTH VADER:
Do not take it lightly when I share this information with you.

APHRA:
Of course, my lord. So very honored, my lord. Does this kid have a name?

A beat of Vader's weighted breathing, then . . .

DARTH VADER:
Luke Skywalker.

APHRA (narration):
Okay, I *totally* heard the dramatic music that time! Something about the way Vader said the kid's name sent a chill up my spine—in a good way. And hey, was that a *first* name to go with that last name I'd never heard of? This was definitely super-important information, and he was sharing it with yours truly.

Score one for Team Me. I was slowly but surely gaining his trust.

Vader cut a striking figure, ebony as the night sky against the interminable blaze of the twin suns of Tatooine. He faced the horizon, his black cape flapping in the driest of winds. Honestly, now I could sort of see the full effect of the cape—sure, it was over the top, but that was the point. It brought the *drama.*

Triple-Zero, Beetee, and I hovered in the background—trying to simultaneously stay out of the way and stay *ready* in case our Dark Lord needed anything.

But ... his utter silence was becoming more frustrating by the minute, so I turned to study the structure he'd brought us to—supposedly, it had once been part of a thriving moisture farm. It was squat, beige, unremarkable. Just like the rest of the planet.

I decided to take my chances and interrupt all the broody staring ...

APHRA:
What are we looking for?

The place is *dead*. It's been dead for weeks. No one alive. Nothing inside.

DARTH VADER:
Skywalker lived here, in this exact spot. He left when his family was ... slain.

TRIPLE-ZERO:
Slain? Oh my, and no organics left in the vicinity ... yet another opportunity I missed while my consciousness was locked away in that horrid vault!

BEETEE:
BLEEEEEEEP!

TRIPLE-ZERO:
Yes, Beetee, that *would* have been fun!

APHRA (narration):
We moved inside the overwhelmingly beige structure, where Vader continued his broody exploration. The inside was about as boring as the outside: bits and pieces of old farming equipment, torn scraps of clothes. The detritus of once vibrant lives cut short.

There were some leftover droid parts that were intriguing—if I'd been on my own, I would have salvaged what I could. Maybe built some more mega-droids. Upon closer inspection, it was clear the place had weathered a fire. Scorch marks everywhere, and all that detritus had a depressing gray cast about it.

And there was something else—

APHRA:
Hmm. Imperial blasters beneath the burns . . .

Your lot were acting covertly here, my lord? Still a little twitchy when the Senate was just fresh in the ground?

DARTH VADER:
I do not require your commentary, Doctor.

APHRA (narration):
That was more of a *question* than a *comment*—but I knew better than to say so. Though I was learning how to be strategic with my queries to Vader, sometimes I still couldn't help but blurt out potentially . . . *provocative* questions at possibly inopportune moments. There are times when I need to know a thing and my overactive brain won't stop spinning until I *do* know the thing. That's why I kept asking my mother why she'd dragged me to Arbiflux, every minute of every day . . . until the day she died.

I never got an answer that satisfied me.

Anyway . . . lucky for me, Triple-Zero had his own observations about all the burnt-out droid husks littering the ground . . .

TRIPLE-ZERO:
Oh my. Such slaughter. Such terrible slaughter . . . These poor droids! Forced to work on this dull moisture farm and now reduced to scrap thanks to careless fleshy ones . . .

APHRA (narration):
I knelt down on the grimy dirt floor, running my fingers over the blaster marks. And I felt a sudden flash of familiarity. This boy—Skywalker—had grown up so much like I had. He probably spent his days wondering what life was like away from this dry, desolate place—what adventures he could have. Why he ended up here.

He must've pestered his parents with the same endless questions.

APHRA:
I guess it's an irony. If the boy was here when the jackboot came down, the Empire would still have the Death Star. But if the family wasn't killed, maybe he'd never have left.

Revenge is one hell of a motivator.

DARTH VADER:
You are correct.

We are too late. Let us move on.

APHRA (narration):
We traveled just a few kilometers away, to the Jundland Wastes, and another small, boring structure that looked like it had recently sustained serious damage.

APHRA:
Assuming Mr. Greatest-Bounty-Hunter-in-the-Galaxy has got his grid refs right, this is where Boba Man, er, Fett fought the boy. And lost.

DARTH VADER:
Wait here until signaled . . .

APHRA (narration):
The Dark Lord entered the structure . . . and then I guess did some of his Force magic stuff? We heard him talking to himself, his deep voice booming off the crumbling walls . . .

TRIPLE-ZERO:
Mistress Aphra, according to my data banks, the act of eavesdropping is considered most impolite!

APHRA:
Exactly, Trip. That's why I'm doing it.

TRIPLE-ZERO:
I knew there was a reason we get on so well, mistress. If I may say so: For an organic, you are not a *complete* waste of space!

APHRA:

Shhh, Trip. Big boss is talking to himself . . .

DARTH VADER:

He fended off the bounty hunter. The boy is *strong* with the Force . . . but with little or no training.

APHRA:

[sotto]

Okay. Interesting?

TRIPLE-ZERO:

I'm not sure our definitions of *interesting* align, mistress.

BEETEE:

BLEEP BLEEP!

APHRA:

Shhh, settle down, you two. I just mean *interesting* in the sense that . . . any information we can gather from observing Lord Vader is information we can also *use* to make ourselves even more valuable to Lord Vader.

TRIPLE-ZERO:

Forgive me, Mistress Aphra, but I am already quite valuable on my own! I am a protocol droid, fluent in—

APHRA:

Shhhhh! He's talking again.

DARTH VADER:

You had twenty years, Obi-Wan. Hiding the boy in the one place I would never return to was cunning, but in this, you are a failure.

APHRA (narration):

Even more interesting? Apparently . . . there was much more to this boy than being a modest farm kid with a weird talent for blowing up Imperial superweapons.

Also? Darth Vader himself had a connection to dusty ol' Tatooine.

More information I could use.

Before I could ruminate further, he emerged . . .

DARTH VADER:
Aphra. I am done. There is *nothing* here.

APHRA:
Great. Where do you want the bomb?

APHRA (narration):
Oh yeah, did I forget to mention? I always have a bomb on me for situations like this. And in this case, I'd broken out my most purely powerful detonator, featuring my own special modifications to make it even more . . . explode-y.

Aphra detonates her bomb, destroying the structure.

APHRA:
Farewell, boring beige structure!

She uses a handheld scanner, which returns a result, and she announces:

APHRA:
Molecular purge is good. As far as forensic science can tell, no one was here, ever.

DARTH VADER:
As I said.

APHRA:
Now what, Lord Vader?

DARTH VADER:
I must return to my duties. I will have a task for you soon enough. It is a matter of some *delicacy.*

SCENE 14. EXT. ROCK CLIMBING FORMATION. UNIVERSITY OF BAR'LETH. DAY. FLASHBACK.

APHRA (narration):
"Delicacy," huh? I mean, we'd already reactivated one of the most dangerous weapons in the galaxy, stolen a precious cybernetic womb from a pissed-off alien queen, and journeyed to the homestead of a possibly Force-sensitive kid who blew up the Death Star.

But *now* things were about to get delicate? Okay.

Despite his penchant for dragging me to musty, burnt-out locations, my new boss continued to be a source of constant fascination.

He was so often secretive, mysterious—downright cryptic.

I get wanting to build your own off-the-grid droid army after you've been reprimanded at work and are trying to put all kinds of secret plans in motion and show the Emperor that you're still *a boss* and should be treated as such. I didn't . . . *quite* get chasing an ex-farm-kid—Force-sensitive or not—through the most desolate places in the Outer Rim.

But like I said: I was learning to be strategic with my questions. Every single scrap of information I was gathering would be important eventually. When I start out on one of my legendary adventures, I don't tend to know how it's all going to turn out—but I *do* know that I'll find my door. There's always that moment where it all comes together, the picture coalesces—and I see, with blazing clarity, where to slide my metaphorical knife so it will hit home.

It was fascinating to observe the Dark Lord's change in moods—sometimes he flipped from his usual mysteriousness to being almost disturbingly forthcoming, revealing stuff to yours truly that was probably at least several levels above my pay grade.

This unpredictability should have been off-putting.

But I loved it. I never knew what the next mission, the next day, the next *hour* was going to hold. And after my stint on Arbiflux, where every *second* was always the same . . . well. This was the kind of adventure I'd been chasing my whole life.

In a weird way, I think my father would have been proud of me. No, I wasn't pursuing the kind of *greatness* he was always going on about. I wasn't trying to bring balance to the universe, or to rediscover some musty old Jedi sect that would somehow usher in a new age of light.

But I was *living*. That was for sure.

And more importantly, after our little quest to Tatooine, I started to feel like Vader was *really* beginning to trust me.

I mean! He told me Skywalker's name. He had me detonate my own special bomb. He let me in on what his Force powers sensed in that beige hut, which seemed very, like . . . *personal*. I know he was talking to himself, but I must presume that he was prepared for me to hear it.

And when he said my next mission would be "a matter of some *delicacy* . . ."

The Dark Lord was letting me into his inner circle, right? I suppose he didn't have much of a circle after the whole Death Star business, but still. I was his trusted circle of *one*. That made me even more important to his greater vision! And that meant I was closer to . . . well. Whatever my endgame was going to be. That moment where I'd know exactly where to slide the knife.

Making yourself invaluable to someone *that* powerful means you're that much closer to grabbing your own power. And I was so ready for that.

Like I said—all these years, I'd been thinking too small.

Who knew that all I needed to truly realize my potential was for someone to *see* it in me. To believe in me and encourage all my initiative-taking!

And then possibly end up on the other side of my metaphorical knife.

I was starting to picture . . . well, a future.

Doctor Chelli Lona Aphra: Super Important Amazing and Extremely Rich Adventurer That Everyone Is Totally Afraid Of.

That sounds *so much better* than Assistant Curator of a Boring-Ass Museum No One Cares About. Take *that,* Utani Xane!

I'd . . . never really pictured a whole *future* before. I have a tendency to not exactly think ahead—not that far. Especially if something presents the possibility of a momentary thrill.

Like when . . . okay, I have to back up for this. Here's the deal, and I'm just going to give it to you straight, because it's highly embarrassing. After our little adventure in the library, I went out of my way to avoid Sana Starros. Because every time I thought of her, those dark eyes and that whiskey voice, I got . . . *mushy.* I thought I had grown past such things, especially since my mother's mushiness was her downfall.

And it's not like things got easier for me after Mom died in that backwater ditch. See, with her dying breath, she called in the Imps, and they shipped me back to my dad—who was still obsessed with Jedi artifacts and his own greatness.

There may have been a . . . small *incident* wherein I tried to burn down his house with all of his research in it.

Maybe it's weird that I decided to become an archaeologist, since my dad's obsession with his work is kind of what destroyed my family. I think I saw it as something I could make *exciting.* It would take me all over the galaxy, away from boring places like Arbiflux.

I never factored mushiness into the equation. Like I said, I was really, really trying not to be like Mom.

But I remember the day the mushiness got the better of me.

I was standing at the base of the university's outdoor climbing formation, a massive wall of jagged rock. It was between classes, and I was all by myself. Students usually opted to scale this perilous structure with a safety harness and cable tethered to their waist—in fact, they were required to.

But I hated that harness. I wanted to feel free. And I'd been waiting for this moment: when I'd be able to sneak out here by myself and finally scale the wall untethered.

My eyes wandered upward to gaze at every harsh angle, every place someone could fall . . .

I felt that *thrill* gather deep in my bones. My heart beat faster as I stepped forward, my gloved hands clamping against the sunbaked rocks.

And I started to climb. My hands grabbed the rocks carefully, methodically. At this point, I practically had the whole formation memorized.

I was nearly at the top—my shirt sticking to my sweaty back, the calluses on my hands pulsating through my protective gloves . . .

And then I heard a voice—*that* voice. Soft, smoky, a little deep . . .

SANA STARROS:
What is that insane woman *doing*?

APHRA (narration):
My head whipped around—and I saw her. She was standing on the ground below, hands on her hips, head cocked to the side. Looking thoroughly perturbed.

SANA STARROS:
Aphra? Is that you? Do you have a death wish or are you just a complete fool?

APHRA (narration):
I . . . *Void,* this next part is *so* humiliating.

I let go. I fell. And I crashed right into Sana Starros, who broke my fall and probably saved me from breaking my neck.

SANA STARROS:
Oof.

APHRA (narration):
"But Chelli," you're saying. "*Why* did you let go?"

That's the humiliating part. I just . . . her voice. Her eyes. Her whole . . . everything. Distracted me. Like they always did.

And then she spoke again.

SANA STARROS:
I don't know if we've *formally* met. I'm Sana Starros. And that was the most reckless, harebrained, absolutely nonsensical—

APHRA:
I know your name.

APHRA (narration):
That's when I kissed her for the first time.

To this day, I don't know why she kissed me back. She always seemed too . . . *sensible* for someone like me. Studious Sana. Perfect, wrinkle-free clothes, nose in a book, always so serious.

But for some reason . . . she threw her common sense out the window. And we were inseparable all through my university days. Right up until . . .

No, we don't need to get into that now.

Recording: Please mark this highly embarrassing sequence for possible deletion. Mark it *as much as you can.*

SCENE 15. EXT. SON-TUUL. DAY.

APHRA (narration):
When Vader contacted me for my next task, it was definitely something only *I* could do. I was eager to rise to the occasion.

And it was—finally, blessedly—on a much nicer planet.

Atmosphere: Serenity. Cool breezes whisper through the trees, accompanied by a babbling brook. In contrast with many of our other locations, this planet bubbles with promise and life.

APHRA (narration):
Son-tuul. A lush, green jungle planet covered with beautiful trees, mountain ranges, and fascinating wildlife. It was the first mission for Vader I'd been sent on all by my lonesome—Triple-Zero and Beetee stayed on the ship as I had to blend in, and their constant commentary about murdering organics was . . . whatever the opposite of *blending in* is. And the Dark Lord had other duties to attend to.

So, yeah. First solo mission! First opportunity to prove that the little bit of trust I'd felt from Vader was warranted.

I was *ready.*

As soon as I stepped onto the surface, I realized that it was . . . quiet. After being surrounded by Trip's ramblings, Beetee's fiery outbursts, and . . . well, all the *noise* that came with working for Darth Vader, it was weird to suddenly be in silence. Nothing but the gentle atmospheric sounds of a planet that *wasn't* a total armpit. A light breeze swept over me, tickling my nostrils with the scent of blooming flowers and the cool water of a nearby creek.

If I were the reflective sort, I probably would have taken a moment to let those lovely scents and sensations wash over me, and to wonder what tiny Chelli Lona Aphra would have thought of all this.

Tiny Chelli Lona Aphra, stuck tending to her patch of dirt while dreaming of wild adventures in systems she couldn't even fathom.

Tiny Chelli Lona Aphra, being used as a convenient mule, carrying her father's dreams in her tiny hands.

Slightly *Less* Tiny Chelli Lona Aphra, stealing rare books from the Bar'leth University Library just to impress a girl.

But since I'm *not* the reflective sort, I didn't do that at all.

I simply checked the coordinates of my destination. There were some really nice bars on Son-tuul.

But I wasn't going to any of those.

SCENE 16. INT. SON-TUUL BAR. LATER.

Atmosphere: Glasses clinking, bar chatter, bets being placed, and—slightly in the distance—the raucous noise of people cheering for a fight about to start. This is the dirtiest, scummiest bar you can imagine, with patrons to match.

APHRA (narration):
No, I had to go to the one with the illegal backroom fighting ring. That's where I was going to find all the individuals of colorful backgrounds and questionable morals that I'd need for my latest mission.

Okay, okay: I *chose* that bar. As a meeting place for my specially selected wretched individuals. I knew that's where they'd feel most at home.

Because it's where *I* felt most at home.

It was one of those establishments where something's *always* skittering around in the cobweb-laden shadows. Where the bar top hasn't been cleaned in millennia, and the resulting crust of grime is so thick, it's basically given you a whole new disgusting surface to set your smeary glass on.

And where the very important business of drinking yourself into oblivion is always getting interrupted by *something*.

I'd barely downed my first drink when the ruckus started. The bouncer was being very *choosy* about who he let inside . . .

SON-TUUL BOUNCER:
I don't think so. Your kind aren't welcome here.

The bouncer lets out a scream as blasterfire hits him square in the chest.

APHRA (narration):
I tossed back the last of my drink and craned my neck toward the entrance, trying to see what was happening.

Of course it was my guys. *Of course.*

Never trust a bunch of bounty hunters to play it cool.

IG-90:
Statement: I have made my point.

APHRA (narration):
IG-90: thoroughly logical assassin droid. And, I'm pretty sure, the one who fired that shot.

BOSSK:
Are you sssssure about that, IG-90? Hissss . . .

APHRA (narration):
Bossk: known Wookiee-killer extraordinaire. Which . . . might be a problem. Since we had a Wookiee on this mission and all.

IG-90:
Query: Where is the Wookiee?

BEEBOX:
He saw there was a pit fight in the back. Dumb lump got nostalgic.

APHRA (narration):
And that's Beebox. Very short. But carries a big gun.

These boys were going to help me carry out my next mission. But I hadn't yet seen the aforementioned "dumb lump"—definitely the linchpin of this adventure.

So I followed them as they headed for the sleaziest part of this sleazy backroom fighting facility. I kept my distance, walking a few paces behind so they wouldn't see me. I wanted to get a sense of how they interacted with each other, how they'd work together. If any of them were prime candidates for tanking our mission before it even started.

Of course the prime candidate for that was the guy in the pit-fight ring.

BLACK KRRSANTAN:
[Wookiee battle roar]

GGGGRRRRRWWWWLLLLLL!

APHRA (narration):
Yup, there he was: Black Krrsantan. Santy and I hadn't engaged in much quality bonding when he'd brought Vader his sniveling bounty. To be fair, we were both pretty busy at the time.

His record, though, was so impressive, I knew he was the right Wookiee for the job. Legend had it that he'd been cast out by his own people for an infraction so mysterious, it was still gossiped about across the galaxy. I was pretty sure it had something to do with stabbing a fellow Wookiee in the back, and I had to appreciate someone with that kind of ice-cold disregard for the bonds of family.

After that, the Xonti Brothers tricked him into becoming an enslaved gladiator, fighting for the crowds. He eventually won his freedom and became a bounty hunter for Jabba the Hutt. From what I'd heard . . . there wasn't much about his old lifestyle, forced to be in the service of unscrupulous gladiatorial entrepreneurs, that he missed.

Except, apparently, the fighting.

He squared off against the other Wookiee in the pit, the motley crowd pressing up against the ring, screaming encouragement.

FIGHT WATCHER #1:
Get him!

FIGHT WATCHER #2:
RIP HIS FUR OFF!

FIGHT WATCHER #1:
A thousand credits on the Wookiee!

BOSSK:
Which one?

IG-90:
Statement: Fights are planned in advance. Query: How is Black Krrsantan a contestant?

BEEBOX:
Good question, IG-90, and I actually have the answer: He strangled the other fighter and stepped in. No one was going to say no. I mean, would you? Bossk?

BOSSK:
I am not that kind of recklesssss, Beebox. Black Krrsantan isss . . . a different ssort. I've captured enough Wookieessss and ssold them to traders to feed the pits. Until Krrsantan, I'd never met one who *volunteered*.

APHRA (narration):
The air was thickening by the second with anticipation. The soupy atmosphere of that back room grew hot and feverish as the crowd thirsted for *blood*.

I studied Krrsantan as he glowered down at the other Wookiee. He was truly massive—I mean, Wookiees are generally massive, but Santy even towered over his unlucky Wookiee opponent. His copious black fur was tangled and knotted but still somehow looked positively majestic—like one of those unruly weeds that grows out in the wildest part of the forest, its leaves spreading until it covers all the neater, more orderly native plants.

The long scar slashed over his left eye pulsed with adrenaline as he sized up his opponent—who was starting to look like he regretted stepping into the ring in the first place.

The fighting pit was somehow even more grime-encrusted than the bar area—of course, part of that was probably due to all the blood, stains old and new smeared over every visible surface. Who knew how *ancient* some of that gore was?

BLACK KRRSANTAN:
[Wookiee battle roar]

RRRRRRRGGRRRRRRWAAAAAAH!

The crowd roars. Black Krrsantan lunges at his opponent . . . and rips off his arm.

APHRA (narration):
Oh . . . Void.

Black Krrsantan throws the arm on the floor of the pit with a mighty whump.

APHRA (narration):
Okay, so this was Santy's technique—don't just rip off your opponent's fur, rip off his whole arm! Gets the fight off to a good start.

In rapid succession, various Wookiee limbs hit the fight-pit floor with a sickening crunch while the crowd cheers.

APHRA (narration):
It was definitely the most . . . appendages I'd ever seen severed during a pit fight.

BLACK KRRSANTAN:
RRRRRAWWWWWRRRRGH!

APHRA (narration):
But that wasn't what made it so riveting.

BOSSK:
Black Krrsantan isss triumphant!

The crowd goes wild.

APHRA (narration):
No. It was the moment right after he won. He looked up from his kill—from that mess of fur and blood and gigantic Wookiee limbs now making a horrendous mess of the pit-fight floor—and his eyes met mine. He gazed at me for a long time, his scar pulsing wildly.

And I felt . . . something.

At the time, I didn't know what it was. Later I'd realize it was . . . connection. Kinship. Instantly *knowing* someone else who's learned how to *survive,* no matter what.

Despite our different, er, hairstyles, in many ways, we were exactly the same.

BEEBOX:
Let's get him a drink. He's always thirsty after beating a guy to death.

APHRA (narration):
Annnnnd . . . that was my cue.

APHRA:
Hey, boys! Of all the scuzzy backroom pit-fighting rings in all the galaxy . . . can you believe we walked into this one?

IG-90:
Statement: I shot my way in.

BOSSK:
You asssked us to meet you here, Aphra. It is hardly a ssssurprise to any of usss.

APHRA:

Spoilsport. Shall we get Santy that drink and discuss my extremely lucrative business proposition?

BLACK KRRSANTAN:

[Wookiee victory roar]

GRRRRWWWWLLLLL!

SCENE 17. INT. SON-TUUL BAR. LATER.

Atmosphere: A more relaxed version of the earlier bar chaos, glasses clinking in celebration. But still with that scummy vibe.

APHRA (narration):
And so, we gathered 'round for a celebratory drink. It was a nice way to build camaraderie amongst this crew of scoundrels.

BLACK KRRSANTAN:
[conversational Wookiee roar]

GRRRRWWWWLLL . . .

BEEBOX:
Yeah, we know. Pit-fight standards have slipped since you quit.

BOSSK:
Doessss it matter? You would have won easily. You always do.

BLACK KRRSANTAN:
[protesting Wookiee roar]

GRRRWOOOLLL!

BEEBOX:
Don't you two start again—I refuse to play peacemaker—

BLACK KRRSANTAN:
[petty Wookiee roar]

RRAAAARRRGOOOOOW!

BEEBOX:
Yes, we all know Bossk has hunted down *a lot* of Wookiees—

BOSSK:
They were bountiessss like any other—I treated them no differently. I am not sssssure why you care, given that you betrayed your own people—

BLACK KRRSANTAN:
GRRRRAWWWWWRRRR!

APHRA:
What did he say? I didn't quite catch the nuance—

BEEBOX:
He said he's not concerned about other Wookiees—he just wants to know that Bossk won't try to double-cross *him*.

BOSSK:
I would not. Unlike sssssome people at thissss table, I believe in upholding the Code at any cost.

BLACK KRRSANTAN:
GRRRRROOOWOWOWOWOLLL!

APHRA:
Okaaay, so did I mention that I need you all to actually *cooperate* for this mission? Everyone's appendages need to still be attached to their bodies by the end of it—and I will be counting, Santy.

BLACK KRRSANTAN:
RRRRAAAAARRRGHHHH!

APHRA:
Quiet down and wipe your mouth. There are ladies present.

Now . . . let's get down to business. Imperial forces have permanently ended the Son-tuul Pride—a criminal organization based right here on beautiful Son-tuul. One of the Hutt Clan's biggest competitors. They're done. Their personal fortune is in transit to its new home in an Imperial vault.

IG-90:

Statement: Everyone knows this.

APHRA:

I know a little *extra*. I know exactly how it's being transported, how to circumvent its guards, and—most of all—how to get away. So, gentlemen and violent robots . . .

Who wants to be rich?

SCENE 18. INT. THE *ARK ANGEL*. SOMEWHERE NEAR ANTHAN PRIME.

APHRA (narration):
You probably noticed that I neglected to mention one tiny little fact to my compatriots. I decided it would be best if my crew of ruthless bounty hunters didn't know Darth Vader was behind the whole operation. First of all, his dark lordliness had entrusted me with a task that involved stealing from the Empire, the people he'd sworn allegiance to. As he'd said . . . it was a matter of *delicacy*. I needed to show him that despite my tornado-like way of dealing with things, I was very trustworthy. Someone who definitely *doesn't* do things like steal extremely valuable books on a whim because she's trying to impress a girl. Or fall off a very high climbing formation because she's *distracted* by a girl. Or . . . never mind, you get the idea.

And yes, I did just use the word *trustworthy* to describe myself— and I can practically see that smug little smile spreading across your face. But in order to use Vader to my best advantage . . . I mean, he *had* to trust me. Fully. And I'd do whatever I had to in order to make that happen.

Something else you should know by now.

Anyway, I thought not letting my gang of scoundrels in on the totality of my plan was also wise because . . . well. Bounty hunters are the worst gossips this side of the Outer Rim. I didn't want them to think there was perhaps a little something more to this mission than "let's all collect a bunch of credits for ourselves and retire, or at least splurge on that solid-gold bowcaster."

But *of course* there was more to it than that.

Perhaps more importantly—people tend to do their best work when they think they're only in it for personal gain. And I needed everybody to do their absolute best work.

Using my very special extra intel—that I definitely did *not* obtain from a certain Dark Lord—we tracked the Imperial cruiser carrying the Son-tuul Pride's fortune to Anthan Prime, located on the very edge of the Outer Rim.

IG-90, Beebox, Bossk, Triple-Zero, and I watched the cruiser navigate around the planet's gaseous atmosphere from the *Ark Angel*.

As for Santy and Beetee . . . they were otherwise engaged. But be patient, I'll get to that in just a bit . . . that's not even the *most* secret part of this plan.

Ugh, I've said too much already!

Back to the Imperial cruiser toting around all that cash . . .

APHRA:
Right. Here they come. I swear, I can see all those credits from here.

IG-90:
Query: Given that it is impossible to "see" the interior of the Imperial cruiser—

APHRA:

Relax, IG-90—it was a joke. An exaggeration. A—

IG-90:

Query—

BOSSK:

No more queriessss. What happens next, Aphra?

APHRA:

When they enter the asteroid belt, we move.

C'mon, *someone* say it!

TRIPLE-ZERO:

Very well, Mistress Aphra. "What asteroid belt?"

BOSSK:

There issss only one asssteroid, asss far asss I can sssee . . .

BEEBOX:

Yes, Aphra, you promised us an *actual* asteroid belt—

IG-90:

Query: The Imperial cruiser is headed for this single asteroid, but that doesn't seem like much of a deterrent—

APHRA:

All right, all right—everyone be quiet now. I really only needed one of you to set that up, now I need just a teeny-weeny beat of anticipatory silence as I hit this big shiny button . . .

Aphra hits a switch on the Ark Angel, *and the single, merry asteroid blows up—creating an asteroid belt.*

TRIPLE-ZERO:

Mistress! Did you just . . . detonate the single asteroid, thereby *creating* an asteroid belt?

APHRA:

Indeed I did, my murderous robot friend! I may or may not have also already fitted said single asteroid with some super-neato explosives. Genius, no?

IG-90:

Statement: It is unclear whether or not this simple action is worthy of the "genius" designation—

BEEBOX:

Yeah, I think that's Aphra's *own* designation, wherein "genius" simply encompasses whatever she's doing at the time.

APHRA:

Wow, really? I start our amazing mission off on a truly explosive note and all the rest of you can do is criticize.

All right, on to step two!

Ion torpedo away!

The ion torpedo hits the Imperial cruiser.

APHRA:

For the next five minutes, the Imperials will think their systems being down is a side effect of the collision. Let's go to work.

SCENE 19. INT. IMPERIAL CRUISER. LATER.

APHRA (narration):
While the Imps were occupied with all those thoroughly distracting explosions I sent their way, my crew did a little space walk on the underside of their cruiser and boarded through an unguarded hatch.

Everything was going exactly to plan. And I was already so impressed with myself! That was some incredible, initiative-taking work!

I mean. Who else would've thought to *create* a whole asteroid belt?

Aphra, Bossk, IG-90, and Beebox land on the floor of the cruiser.

BEEBOX:
We're in.

IG-90:
Statement: Obviously.

BEEBOX:
No need to be rude, metalhead—

IG-90:

Statement: My programming does not allow for anything designated as "rude"—

BOSSK:

Clearly it doessss, IG-90.

APHRA:

Okay, okay—cool it with the bounty hunter banter! Remember, I said we need to end this mission with everyone's limbs intact!

IG-90:

Statement: Beebox started it.

APHRA:

Ignoring that. Let's see, the vault is . . . somewhere.

Beebox, that door leads to the crew's quarters. Keep it sealed. Make sure it looks like a localized malfunction.

BEEBOX:

Order me like an astrobot again, and you'll get a slug through your head. I know what I'm doing.

APHRA:

In ten minutes' time, you'll all be able to make a *house* out of credit ingots, Beebox. I'd suggest not killing me before that.

Now. Let's all get ready—expect contact with vault security in three, two . . .

There's a sudden flurry of blasts from a trio of Viper droids guarding the vault.

APHRA:

Okay, the Viper droids are ahead of schedule. But at least now we know where the vault is!

BOSSK:

Hard to believe Imperialsss ussse droids for work like thisss. Obsssolete.

IG-90:

Interjection: Offensive.

BOSSK:

You're an IG. Not the sssame.

APHRA:

The Imperial stormtroopers' pension scheme isn't exactly market leading, Bossk. They're not letting anyone with anything other than a program in their head anywhere near the rich stuff.

BOSSK:

It sstill doesn't make senssse—

IG-90:

Statement: On the contrary, Viper droids are actually quite suited to a number of tasks—

BEEBOX:

This conversation is unnecessary—

APHRA:

Aw, Beebox, it's all right—we need to have a little fun, here! And speaking of fun, I've got something very special prepared for our best Viper droid friends—

BEEBOX:

What's that?

APHRA:

You interrupted my big reveal! It's an electromagnetic pulse grenade that I've elevated with just a dash of extra juice.

BEEBOX:

Extra *what*?

APHRA:

Get ready, and . . . bombs away!

Aphra rolls an electromagnetic pulse grenade toward the feet of the Viper droids. It explodes in spectacular fashion.

APHRA:

[shouting over the explosions]

Okay, boys, shoot everything you can!

Bossk and IG-90 fire on the droids while Aphra scrambles over to the vault.

APHRA:

And I'll do the vault part since that requires *my* expertise. We've only got a couple more minutes before the Imps get the door open.

BOSSK:

Ssss. Let them.

APHRA:

Murder on your own time, Bossk. If we let them through, we have to blow the ship to cover our traces. We need to make sure no one knows we were ever here . . .

Now keep shooting up those droids and let me *work*.

Oh, hello, Vault. Don't you look absolutely *beautiful*.

APHRA (narration):

I know we were in a high-stress situation here, but communing with that big shiny vault forced my mind to completely *relax*. It was like the rest of the room—in all its shoot-'em-up glory—disappeared and it was just me and the vault, that special mechanical language passing between us until it agreed to open up to me.

There's just something about that moment when you hear the telltale click. Maybe because it feels like . . . the vault is trusting me with its deepest, darkest secrets.

Or maybe, in this case, it was because there was a truly disgusting amount of credits on the other side.

Anyway, tempting as it was, my goal this time actually *wasn't* to crack the vault open.

Oh, what? You're confused by that? "Chelli," you're saying. "What . . . is this plan? And exactly how many parts of it are secret? Is this all some sort of elaborate ploy for you to keep all those credits for yourself? But then . . . why wouldn't you crack the safe?"

Jeez, what's with all the super-nosy questions? Don't you trust me to—actually, scratch that, you totally *shouldn't* trust me. You shouldn't even trust me to tell my own story right. You *should,* however, know that I'm not a dirty double-crosser set on using a bunch of willing suckers to steal all that cash and then keep it for myself. Shame on you for even thinking that! I mean, when working with bounty hunters, you have to uphold at least *some* aspects of the Code.

Anyway . . . this part, the bit with the vault, I really only kept a secret from *you,* dear listener. And that was only so I could tell you what I was up to at the most dramatic moment possible! When things are going crash-bang-boom!

But rest assured: The boys knew what I was doing.

My heart was beating a zillion miles a minute as I planted a homing beacon—another one of my special creations, with just a little extra juice—on the vault. That prepared it for the next step of my brilliant plan . . .

APHRA:
And now with the homer set, let's run for our lives.

Triple-Zero—tell that big hairy lump he can start his run.

TRIPLE-ZERO (on comm):
Very good, Mistress Aphra.

Mr. Krrsantan—Mistress Aphra informs me you can begin . . .

BLACK KRRSANTAN (on comm):
GRRROWWWWLLLLLLL!

APHRA (narration):
Oh, I didn't tell you about this part, either! But don't worry, the boys all knew about this, too. Can you please stop thinking the absolute worst of me? I do have *some* honor.

See, here's where Santy came in. As the rest of us skedaddled back to the *Ark Angel,* he piloted his gunship through my incredible fake asteroid belt, shooting out a cable to lasso one of the asteroids. Then—boom!—he rammed that asteroid into the Imperial cruiser, cracking open the vault.

That's right: We broke into the vault from the *other* side. *From space.*

I know. I *know.* Sometimes I impress *myself,* even.

I gazed out into space as we space-walked our way along the underside of the Imperial cruiser. Credit ingots spilled out into the starscape—an ingot belt to rival the asteroid belt, shiny and beautiful and so very, very expensive.

The ingots spill out into space—and there are millions of them.

APHRA (narration):
They glittered as they floated through the stars, their surfaces like rainbow prisms.

And even though we were too far away to actually see this . . . I thought, just for a moment, that I could see my face reflected in their multicolored surfaces. My eyes sparked with the excitement of adventure, the triumph of a mission accomplished. And I was *beaming,* that triumph surging through my veins like wildfire.

Hell, I'll say it: In that moment, right after accomplishing my first solo mission for Darth Vader . . . I felt *great.* I could finally, in a way, see why my father had chased that feeling so hard, why he'd completely neglected his wife and only child in pursuit of making his mark. It was absolutely intoxicating—exhilaration and pride and the call of all those credits swirling through my bloodstream in a heady mix.

And as the ingot belt shimmered its way across this little patch of galaxy . . . I just *let* myself feel that. And I tried to somehow beam that feeling through time, back to Tiny Chelli Lona Aphra and her dusty chatterplants.

Someday, I thought to her, *someday you will be* more. *And all of this will have been worth it.*

SCENE 20. INT. THE *ARK ANGEL*. MOMENTS LATER.

TRIPLE-ZERO:
Welcome back to the *Ark Angel,* Mistress Aphra. Black Krrsantan's asteroid appears to have successfully penetrated the hull. The ingots and all evidence you were ever there is jettisoning into space. It's rather pretty, though it is a shame no humanoids were harmed—

APHRA:
Not the time, Trip. Now, if I've calculated this right, Beetee will do the rest. Anyone with fingers, cross 'em. And hope that Beetee can generate enough of a field to scoop up the loot.

TRIPLE-ZERO:
I'm confident he can, mistress—Beetee is quite resourceful.

APHRA:
That's what I'm counting on, Trip. Because losing several kerzillion credits into space would put a downer on the day.

APHRA (narration):
Oh yes. That was another part of my brilliant plan—Beetee generated a magnetic field, containing as many of the credits as he could.

Of course . . . it wasn't *all* the credits. There were just *so* many.

So we had to watch a bunch of them float away, like an ominous storm cloud of money. I can't say that didn't hurt, and Tiny Chelli Lona Aphra probably would've been disappointed in me for that. But once we got all the credits Beetee *did* manage to save on board the *Ark Angel* . . . it was still impressive. Piles and piles of shiny ingots as far as the eye could see, their brilliant surfaces throwing so many colors around the room.

But, given that my team consisted of a bunch of ruthless bounty hunters . . . they weren't entirely satisfied.

BEEBOX:
Are we rich?

APHRA:
We're rich . . . *er.*

BEEBOX:
That is *not* what you promised, Aphra!

BLACK KRRSANTAN:
GRRRAAAARRRGGHHHHH!

APHRA:
C'mon . . . do you all really need to *glare* at me like that? Math was *hard.* There were a lot of variables we just didn't know—and a plan of this magnitude, this brilliance, required a lot of moving parts. Beetee still generated a pretty big field—

BOSSK:
Hisss. Not big enough.

BEEBOX:
Yes, and we really don't need to keep hearing about the brilliance of your plan, Aphra—especially since it resulted in such a middling payoff.

BLACK KRRSANTAN:
[agreeing]

RAAAAAWWWWWR!

APHRA:
It's still a score. It's still a *huge* score.

IG-90:
Statement: It could have been huger.

APHRA:
Cheer up, IG-90. We've ripped off the Empire and they don't know we were even here. Which *is* pretty brilliant.

IG-90:
Statement: Beebox is right. The "brilliance" of said plan is irrelevant if the result is unsatisfactory.

BOSSK:
Agreed!

BLACK KRRSANTAN:
RAWR!

APHRA:
Look, if this giant avalanche of credits is just too measly for y'all, I'll be glad to take it off your hands—

IG-90:
Statement: Do that and die.

BLACK KRRSANTAN:
RAAAAWR!

BEEBOX:
[resigned]

Krrsantan is right—better to have something than nothing. And there's no such thing as easy credits. Let's carve this Naboo pond fowl up.

APHRA:
Glad to see you coming around to my amazingness, Beebox— I knew you were my favorite.

BEEBOX:
That's not what I said—

APHRA:

[interrupts]

I fronted the cash for all the equipment. I take expense, then divide
by . . .

*The bounty hunters immediately arm their weapons and point
them at Aphra.*

BLACK KRRSANTAN:

[protesting Wookiee roar]

KRRRROOOOWWWWWWWWL!

BOSSK:

I don't think sssssoooooo . . .

APHRA:

Okay, okay. Expenses will be taken from *my* back end.

BOSSK:

Hissssss. Better.

APHRA:

You guys are *not* team players.

BLACK KRRSANTAN:

GRRROOOWWWWWLLL.

BEEBOX:

Yeah, the Wookiee's right. You better not have crossed us, Aphra.

IG-90:

Statement: You can't hide from bounty hunters.

TRIPLE-ZERO:

Strictly speaking, you can hide, it just tends to be ineffective. Running is statistically better, but only fractionally.

APHRA:

Comic murderous pedantry aside, the droid's right. You all know
I've got a fairly lax attitude to property rights, but do you think I'd
cross *four* of the deadliest bounty hunters in the galaxy?

IG-90:

Statement: Yes.

BOSSK:

I think you'd *think* about it. Then sslink away.

APHRA:

Sooooo . . . do this again soon, sometime? My employer has more work coming up.

BEEBOX:

Next time you pay up front, Aphra.

APHRA:

You know, Beebox . . . I'll see what I can do.

SCENE 21. INT. CAVE. ANTHAN 13, MOON OF ANTHAN PRIME. LATER.

APHRA (narration):
Next stop: Anthan 13, a moon of Anthan Prime. I'd sent the bounty hunter gang on their merry way, so it was just me, Triple-Zero, and Beetee, camped out in a dark, shadowy cave replete with jagged rock formations throwing monstrous shadows everywhere.

So cold! So dark! So *mysterious.* Can't you just hear the mysterious, uh . . . wind! Whistling through . . .

Atmosphere: A mysterious-sounding wind whistles through the cave. Perhaps the soundscape is slightly exaggerated here, to reflect Aphra's telling of it.

APHRA (narration):
Oooooh, scary! The perfect atmosphere for a *grand reveal.* Like one of those rock formations revealing itself to be an actual monster jumping out of the shadows!

Or . . . an unexpected bit of light filtering into all that darkness. Beautiful, beautiful light . . . emanating directly from *the massive pool of ingots* dumped in the cave's center.

Whoa.

It was such an endless sea of credits, you could have jumped in and had yourself a little swim, if you were into that sort of thing.

TRIPLE-ZERO:
Well, Mistress Aphra, *this* is *quite* the bounty. Perhaps the bounty hunters would have been less *enraged* if you had simply shared *all* of the ingots with them.

APHRA:
Shhh, Trip. Just let me enjoy this for a minute.

APHRA (narration):
Oh, what, you're confused again? Did you really think I'd let all those beautiful ingots slip off into space like that? Do you know me *at all*?

Nah, there was always another twist to my grand ol' heist plan.

Remember how I said there were things I wasn't telling you? And . . . well, most of those things, the bounty hunter boys knew about. But this one . . . they didn't.

Recording: Rewind to previously encrypted section six-eight-eight. Right after Black Krrsantan's epic, limb-crushing pit fight.

Passcode: APHRA KNOWS YOU ARE A FOOL AND WILL TOTALLY FALL FOR ANYTHING seven-five-nine.

We hear the sound of the recording rewinding itself to the correct spot.

SCENE 22. INT. SON-TUUL BAR. FLASHBACK.

Atmosphere: The rowdy sounds of the crowd post-pit-fight.

BLACK KRRSANTAN:
[triumphant]

GRAAAAAAAARGHHHHHH!

APHRA:
Hey. Psst. Santy. Before we go get that drink with our scummy compatriots . . . let's have a little one-on-one bonding time.

BLACK KRRSANTAN:
Grrrr?

APHRA:
When I saw you across the way, pulling off that guy's arms . . . well, I felt something. Something real. You could perhaps call it a . . . kinship?

BLACK KRRSANTAN:
GRAGH!

APHRA:

Yes, yes, I'm aware that us being related is very likely a biological impossibility. What I meant was: On the inside, once you get past my strikingly lovely face and all your matted fur . . . we're the same. We both always dive headfirst into a fight, even if there's a possibility we'll end up with slightly fewer appendages. We don't care. We're always chasing that *thrill*.

BLACK KRRSANTAN:

RAAAAAAARWR!

APHRA:

Wait, don't walk away from me! I . . . I . . . look. I *know* you. After you won, I could see it in your eyes.

You're a *survivor*.

And so am I.

And I have a way that we could both survive . . . a little better?

BLACK KRRSANTAN:

[I'm listening]

Graawr rawr?

APHRA:

Right. Okay. So. This mission involves us cracking into an Imperial cruiser safe and liberating a bunch of credits into the unforgiving expanse of space.

Space, Santy!

BLACK KRRSANTAN:

[get on with it!]

Raaawr!

APHRA:

Okay, okay, I'm getting to that! Don't kill me for attempting to tell this extra-dramatic-like. I'm trying to entertain you here.

I'm thinkin': These other bozo bounty hunters will be perfectly happy with a . . . slightly lesser take. So what if I send you, on your own ship, out to gather up all of those spacefaring credits—but we only give them *some* of the take.

The bulk of it . . . well, you'll deposit that directly into this glorious cave I have waiting on Anthan 13.

BLACK KRRSANTAN:
GRAAAARGH!

APHRA:
I dunno, you figure out that part! Why do I have to do everything?

BLACK KRRSANTAN:
[thoughtful]

Grrrar argh?

APHRA:
Using a satellite-type situation sounds perfect! And I have a droid who can help with generating the magnetic field. See, Santy, I knew you were the perfect person to help me with my brilliant plan! And make it even brilliant . . . er.

BLACK KRRSANTAN:
GRRAAAARGH!

APHRA:
I know. I've been through a lot, too, and . . . well.

[beat, and then her voice turns sincere—for once]

What the Xonti Brothers did to you . . . what all of those people did to you. It wasn't right.

BLACK KRRSANTAN:
RAARRGH ARGH?

APHRA:

You want me to help you with something else? Well . . . okay, let's hear it . . .

APHRA (narration):

Recording: Jump back to the part in the cave on Anthan 13—you know, me enjoying all of my new riches . . .

SCENE 23. INT. CAVE. ANTHAN 13, MOON OF ANTHAN PRIME.

We hear the recording fast-forwarding back to the correct spot.

APHRA (narration):
Okay, so I *am* a dirty double-crosser set on using a bunch of willing suckers to steal all that cash and then keep it for myself!

You know me way better than you think you do.

I mean, I didn't keep it *all*. They got *something*. But they surely could have gotten a whole lot more . . .

APHRA:
Just look at the way it sparkles . . .

TRIPLE-ZERO:
Would this be the time to confess I always had a hankering to be coated in a precious metal, Mistress Aphra?

APHRA:
We all have our unfulfilled desires, Trip. Staying hungry forces us to strive for personal betterment.

TRIPLE-ZERO:
Goodness! Do you really believe that?

APHRA:
Of course not. But there's no way you're getting any of the sparkly, sorry. And anyway, I think you're beautiful the way you are.

TRIPLE-ZERO:
Well, Mistress Aphra, now I'm feeling *extra* unfulfilled.

APHRA:
For the moment, you'll have to stay that way. Our best bounty-huntin' pal should be here any minute . . .

BLACK KRRSANTAN:
GRROWWWWWWLLL!

APHRA:
Santy! There you are. I know your previous career had you in front of a crowd, but I didn't know you were *that* good an actor. Remind me never to play cards with you.

BLACK KRRSANTAN:
GRRRWAAAAR!

APHRA:
Yeah, it's five times your score. And I'll help you with your other problem—the thing we talked about.

BLACK KRRSANTAN:
RRROOOOWWWWWL!

APHRA:
Yeah, yeah, I *do* like my arms attached to my body. We're in this together. Cross three bounty hunters? Sure. Four? Even I'm not that suicidal.

But, hey: Pleasure working with you, eh? And I almost never say that. Well. I almost never *mean* it.

BLACK KRRSANTAN:
[a pleasure for me, too . . .]

RAAAWR!

APHRA (narration):
As he lumbered off, struggling under the weight of all his treasure, our eyes met once more. And I felt that pulse of familiarity again. That *knowing*.

I *knew* why he kept volunteering for these brutal fights. Why he was constantly chasing these risks that came with no reward—except the possibility of immediate death.

He hungered for the sheer thrill of it. He needed to *feel* it, deep down in his oversized Wookiee bones.

He needed to feel himself . . . surviving.

I understood that.

I knew I'd see him again. I wondered if our eyes would meet in the same way. I wondered if he knew I'd meant a lot of what I'd said to him—and that I hardly ever mean anything I say.

Don't . . . say anything. I know what you're thinking. And I . . . well, maybe I should say this *now* . . .

The recording turns fuzzy.

APHRA (narration):
Recording: Delete that last bit. It's boring and no one cares.

Let's talk about something more scintillating! After Santy took off, it didn't take Vader long to show up. I was eager to dazzle him with all I'd managed to accomplish on my first solo mission.

We hear Vader's telltale breathing . . .

APHRA:
Hey, boss, nice to see ya. I promised the Wookiee help with finding the people responsible for enslaving him and cutting him up. Any chance of helping me out?

DARTH VADER:
We will see.

APHRA:
Okay, I'll take it. Now ... we have a droid factory. We have the bounty hunters. We have the money to *pay* the bounty hunters. What's next?

Is it a holiday? I think I'm due a little holiday time.

DARTH VADER:
I need certain information confirmed. From one who is proving elusive.

APHRA:
That kid who destroyed the Death Star—Skywalker?

DARTH VADER:
Not yet. First *this*.

APHRA (narration):
You see what I mean about alternating between wildly secretive and mind-blowingly forthcoming? Anyway. He handed me a datachip—and gave me a name.

And one more bit of information, something he *really* wanted to know about.

But I'll get to that in due time.

DARTH VADER:
Contact me only when you have succeeded. If you do not contact me within a month, I will contact *you*.

That is not something you would enjoy.

APHRA (narration):
And with that ... he was gone. Leaving me once again with no company but my killer robots.

Oh, and all my money.

Normally, the money would've been the main thing I took pleasure in. But this time . . . there was something more. I could tell I'd impressed him. I'd impressed *Darth Vader*.

I'd done something only I could do, and I'd done it *well*. I'd showed him that there was only one Chelli Lona Aphra: rogue archaeologist, excellent heister and double-crosser . . . and supposedly totally loyal to him. Perhaps the ultimate double cross?

I'd proved to him that my brilliance was no fluke, that I could get things done and keep all of his secrets.

And now he was entrusting me with even more of them.

I was getting closer to discovering the cracks in his armor, I could feel it—and that gave me an even bigger thrill than stealing all those credits.

Of course, Trip had to interrupt my nice moment with more of his complaining . . .

TRIPLE-ZERO:
Mistress Aphra, when Mr. IG-90 received a share of the spoils, I couldn't help but take my continuing poverty somewhat personally . . .

APHRA:
You take your joy in work.

TRIPLE-ZERO:
I was not locked in a room with a humanoid and a sharp implement, Mistress Aphra. There was little "joy."

APHRA:
Patience, Triple-Zero. In this outfit, it can only be a matter of time.

SCENE 24. INT. GAMBLING PARLOR. THE SPIRE.
ANTHAN PRIME. DAY.

APHRA (narration):
Naturally, Vader gave me basically no information regarding the decryption of this mysterious datachip. I knew that it contained information on someone called Commodex Tahn, and that Vader thought Tahn might possess some vital knowledge.

And . . . yeah, there was that one other thing I haven't told you yet. Having to do with what that "vital knowledge" might entail. Be patient.

Anyway, this was just another opportunity to prove my brilliance.

With Triple-Zero and Beetee in tow, I jetted over to Anthan Prime, where we stopped off at the Anthan Spire—a glittering floating city of excess that houses a holiday resort for the hyper-rich. At least up top. The fancy folks in charge took one look at the *Ark Angel* and suggested we park somewhere more our speed—the tradesperson's entrance.

We docked in the lower area, where, it must be said, there was still plenty of flash—mostly in the form of high-stakes gambling.

Atmosphere: The whir, hum, and melodic "dings" of a bustling gambling parlor. Controlled chaos. This is a place of excess, of the wealthy indulging in their every whim. It has an opulent sheen the grimy Son-tuul bar did not—but of course there's a seediness lurking just beneath the surface.

TRIPLE-ZERO:

Oh, holo-chess! Beautiful holo-chess! It's been a while!

BEETEE:

BLEEP!

TRIPLE-ZERO:

Yes, I have been locked in storage for years. That is "a while."

APHRA:

Are you any good?

TRIPLE-ZERO:

My specialties are etiquette, customs, translation, and torture. A lot of nonessential protocol droid programming was jettisoned to fit that last one in. So, no. I'm terrible, Mistress Aphra. But I do love it so.

BEETEE:

BLEEP BLEEP!

TRIPLE-ZERO:

Yes, Beetee, I suppose I am a terribly sore loser.

APHRA:

Well, maybe after this, we'll all get that holiday we deserve. Think of it, Trip: You could get plated in precious metal at the fancy droid spa while gambling the rest of your payday away . . .

TRIPLE-ZERO:

Oooh, sounds like the perfect opportunity for a little light torture as well!

BEETEE:
BLEEEEEP!

TRIPLE-ZERO:
True, Beetee: If we're on holiday, I should indulge myself. Extensive torture, it is!

Now, Mistress Aphra, are you serious about that payday, because as we'd discussed previously—

APHRA:
Shhh, Trip, I need to concentrate—gotta get in the right mindset to see an old friend . . .

TRIPLE-ZERO:
Which "old friend" is this, Mistress Aphra, and are you certain you can classify them as such? You seem to use the term *friend* rather . . . loosely.

BEETEE:
BLEEEEEEP!

TRIPLE-ZERO:
Yes, Beetee, but I was trying to put it a bit more diplomatically . . .

APHRA:
It's a guy named The Ante—if anyone can unlock Vader's datachip, it's him . . .

And yeah, we're friends.

Basically.

APHRA (narration):
I let Triple-Zero and Beetee hang back while I approached The Ante—he was settled into a spacious nook just off of the gambling parlor, watching various statistics and gaming status reports fly by on a wide expanse of glowing monitors. And he was sitting in one of those giant chairs that spins around—for extra dramatic effect, I guess. There's really no other reason to have a chair that purely ostentatious.

The Ante swiveled around in that giant chair and regarded me through the inky black pits he calls eyes. His head looked a bit like a humanoid skeleton that's been left out in the sun too long, and his voice had a harsh, raspy quality.

When he spoke, the effect was always . . . disconcerting. To say the least.

APHRA:
Ah, greetings, Mr. Ante. It's been a while, and now it's time to *up* the ante—specifically *my* ante.

THE ANTE:
First, that's "*The* Ante." Secondly, it's been a long, long time since you could afford my rates, Aphra, but now you've cleared your slate.

What are you looking for? And before you start . . . I stress I have a *lot* of information about some particularly elusive individuals.

APHRA:
I know. Anything worth knowing has passed through that big bald brain of yours.

We need to know about an individual called Commodex Tahn. This datachip has everything we've got.

Aphra hands the chip to The Ante.

APHRA (narration):
The Ante popped the chip into one of his gigantic computers—and a web of information popped up immediately. The Ante's face lit up—he looked like me gazing upon all those beautiful ingots in the cave. We all have our true passions—and often those passions can be translated into weaknesses.

I always like to know what people's weaknesses . . . er, *passions* are. Even when they're my friends.

Actually, *especially* when they're my friends.

We hear the whir of something being run through a computer.

THE ANTE:

Hmm . . . Are you *sure* this is the right guy? He doesn't seem particularly interesting.

APHRA:

No, he's the one. Give me everything you've got.

THE ANTE:

The client is always right. Done.

Beeps and whistles as information is transferred. A holo activates.

APHRA:

Distinguished looking.

THE ANTE:

I suppose. There are *no* refunds.

APHRA:

Thanks for this, The Ante. Always a pleasure.

Aphra dumps a whole mess of credits on top of one of The Ante's computers.

THE ANTE:

Aphra, you've just spent a *lot* of money to get information you could probably have found through official records . . .

APHRA:

I did. But you're faster and far more discreet.

THE ANTE:

That I am. But I have to wonder: Who could possibly be interested in someone like this? Tahn was a military clerk in the Republic era, before leaving service and entering the rather dull family business upon the death of his father. Retired now for nearly twenty years.

APHRA:

What family business?

A few beeps, holo shifts.

THE ANTE:
See for yourself . . .

APHRA:
[reading the information]

Huh. Looks like they were morticians.

On *Naboo.*

SCENE 25. EXT. COMMODEX TAHN'S HOME. NABOO. NIGHT.

Atmosphere: The most serene evening you can imagine. Total, luxurious peace—which Aphra is about to destroy.

APHRA (narration):
Naboo. Didn't I mention wanting to go here at one point? I guess I was imagining something more along the lines of lounging by one of those famous lakes while aesthetically pleasing humanoids brought me cocktails.

Instead, we arrived under the cover of night. That's really the only way to go when you're trying to surprise someone.

How interesting to see that our new best friend, Commodex Tahn, retired mortician of Naboo, was living out his golden years in a sprawling-yet-tasteful luxury villa. I suppose he felt like he deserved it after all the years of service to his people: peace and quiet, serenity, and the joy of silence. All of this emanated off of the gorgeous marble columns of the house, the spacious balcony that looked out onto the crystal-clear darkness of the night sky.

We were about to completely mess all of that up.

I don't know if you've ever commanded your very own platoon of commando droids that you manufactured from an alien queen's robot womb that you kind of, sort of stole from her, but let me tell you: It's a *rush*.

They marched into the place in formation, ready to totally destroy the perfect serenity Commodex Tahn had taken such pains to craft.

And of course, I had my two most important battle droids by my side—we hung back while the commandos stormed the place. But I knew I'd eventually need Trip and Beetee's special talents—especially when Tahn pulled out a blaster rifle and started firing on my precious commandos . . .

We hear explosions of gunfire.

TRIPLE-ZERO:
Oh dear! It sounds as though our commando droid brethren are having some difficulties. Your specific talents are needed, Beetee!

BEETEE:
BLEEP BLEEP!

TRIPLE-ZERO:
You don't have to be so rude—I was paying you a compliment!

APHRA:
Remember, guys: *Stun.* No killing! We need him *alive.*

BEETEE:
BLEEEEEEEEP!

TRIPLE-ZERO:
Yes, Beetee. Mistress Aphra means "alive" as in "alive until we have a little chat with him." Won't that be fun? Oh my, I haven't gotten to torture anyone in so long!

APHRA:
It hasn't been *that* long—what about that poor soul Santy delivered to Vader?

TRIPLE-ZERO:

Oh, mistress, that feels like it was positively *ages* ago!

If my programming allowed me to tremble with excitement, I think I would.

BEETEE:

BLEEP BLEEP BLEEP!

TRIPLE-ZERO:

Yes, Beetee: Propel yourself onto the balcony, and Mistress Aphra and I will follow!

Beetee propels himself onto Tahn's balcony.

COMMODEX TAHN:

Get away from me, droid!

Tahn shoots at Beetee, who fires back with an explosion.

COMMODEX TAHN:

Argh!

BEETEE:

BLEEP! BLEEP!

APHRA:

Beetee! I said *stun*!

TRIPLE-ZERO:

With the greatest respect, Mistress Aphra, the most important part of your order was "alive." Beetee is very much a big-picture sort of thinker. And his big picture primarily consists of organics getting shot.

BEETEE:

BLEEP! BLEEP!

APHRA:

Enough! Find whatever safe he has. Get it open. Beetee, clean it out. We need to make this look like a robbery.

TRIPLE-ZERO:

An excellent strategy, Mistress Aphra! Perhaps, depending on what's in the safe, we could once again discuss the matter of my payment—

APHRA:

Not now, Trip.

COMMODEX TAHN:

So you're going to kill me no matter what I do. You're not giving me much motivation to help, miss.

APHRA:

I'm sorry. But that's not going to be something you have any say in, Commodex Tahn.

COMMODEX TAHN:

Commodex who?

APHRA:

There's a plaque right here on your wall that says PRESENTED TO COMMODEX TAHN FOR SERVICES TO NABOO BY PADMÉ AMIDALA. If you're going to lie, you need to try harder than that.

COMMODEX TAHN:

If you don't want money, then what do you want? I'm old, I'm retired—living out my golden years in peace. I don't mean anyone any harm—

APHRA:

You're Commodex Tahn. You prepared Senator Amidala's body for burial. We need your fond, nostalgic memories of that sad time.

COMMODEX TAHN:

If you knew her, you wouldn't speak so. I won't betray her.

She was a great queen. A *good* queen.

APHRA:

A good queen? I guess a good queen is a good thing. But I'd take strong over good any day.

COMMODEX TAHN:
"The ends justify the means," is that what you're saying? Easy to say when you're not the means.

APHRA:
Ptth. When you were playing courtier on Naboo, I was trying to grow up living in a galactic war. I had a mom who pretended we weren't.

COMMODEX TAHN:
I was hardly "playing courtier," my position involved many important duties and services—

APHRA:
Shh. I'm talking now. And you're listening.

However you want to slice it, you lived a life of luxury and privilege, sir.

Meanwhile, I was growing up in a dead-end homestead on the frontier, a brave spiritual life on a new world my mom dragged me to after a split from Dad.

COMMODEX TAHN:
Your mother just wanted a better life for you, it sounds like.

APHRA:
Well, that's not what we got—either of us. Here's the thing with wars—if the war doesn't get you, all the scum opportunists profiting from the chaos will.

Raiders came in. Mom told me to run. I did.

COMMODEX TAHN:
You survived.

APHRA:
You bet I did.

And then . . . I came back with this awesome cannon I found in a cave I was exploring and blew them all to pieces.

I saved everyone.

COMMODEX TAHN:
You see, you survived worse than—

APHRA:
And Dad came back, we all lived happily ever after. And now I spend my time wandering the galaxy recovering awesome cannons.

My mom *definitely* didn't die in a ditch on a dead-end forest world we only went to because she was so idealistic.

COMMODEX TAHN:
I'm sorry.

APHRA:
Weren't you listening? There was a war going on. Everyone has a sob story.

Boo-hoo for everyone.

Point being—if you're not a strong queen, good doesn't mean *anything*. And strong and order beats good but weak on every planet in the galaxy, from now until the end of time.

COMMODEX TAHN:
Amidala was good *and* strong.

APHRA:
Not strong enough.

Triple-Zero? Get him talking.

TRIPLE-ZERO:
At once, Mistress Aphra. And might I just say, that was a very stirring speech, I agree entirely with your points about—

APHRA:
Not now, Trip. Please. Just do your job, okay?

Aphra wanders to the edge of the balcony as Triple-Zero moves in on Tahn.

TRIPLE-ZERO:

Do you have much experience with torture, Commodex? I don't imagine that being a mortician put you in the line of fire very often. Then again: You know everyone's secrets. You quite literally know where all the bodies are buried.

COMMODEX TAHN:

You're not getting anything from me. I still have loyalty to the queen.

TRIPLE-ZERO:

Oh, you are just adorable.

I love it when you play your part.

Triple-Zero reaches a hand—already crackling with electricity—toward Tahn.

COMMODEX TAHN:

No . . . no . . . *nooooooooooo!*

SCENE 26. INT. LIVING ROOM. COMMODEX TAHN'S HOME. MOMENTS LATER.

APHRA (narration):
As Tahn continued to scream in pain under Trip's ministrations, I wandered to another part of the house. I like to give people space to work.

Tahn's home may have been luxurious and beautifully appointed, but it wasn't cold and sterile the way so many luxurious, beautifully appointed homes are. The walls were lined with holos of Tahn amongst friends and family, their happy faces beaming out at him every morning when he took his caf.

There was so much warmth in those pictures. Camaraderie.

I bet you're imagining me gazing at these and falling into a melancholy, reflective mindset, where I go deep into my softest feelings and feel all sad about the fact that I don't have a bunch of my own super-smiley holos to display.

First of all: I don't have "soft" feelings. I barely have *feelings*. And I don't tend to forge lasting bonds of . . . anything. Those kinds of bonds make you scream out in terror right before you die. Because you can't bear the thought of being separated from the people you love so much it *hurts*.

That's the way my mom screamed, right before she bit it. She revealed her true self, the one behind the brave, pioneer woman homesteader. And her true self was *weak*.

Did you like my . . . *embellishment* of that story, by the way? Personally, I think it works much better—who doesn't love an intrepid child hero, fighting her way back to her mother and taking out all the bad guys? It's the stuff fairy tales are made of.

I touched a particularly jolly-looking holo, Tahn beaming from the middle of a crush of people who appeared to be his family.

I wondered if he was currently feeling what my mother felt, right before she died. If he was scared. As my fingers brushed against his smiling face, that holo slid to the side, and a different one popped up. A very beautiful woman, sleeping—close on her face, the better to see her elegant features. Her long brown curls were festooned with colorful blooms, her face was serene . . . and then I realized, she wasn't sleeping. She was dead.

This was Padmé Amidala. The good queen. At her funeral.

I touched the holo again—and it fritzed.

And then suddenly her voice filled the room.

PADMÉ AMIDALA (recording):
Commodex Tahn—I hope this message finds you well. I . . . I'm afraid. I do not like to admit that so baldly. Forgive me for this momentary weakness, but the situation is dire and I cannot see the light. Please tell no one of this, I do not want the good people of Naboo to think of their former queen and senator as someone who forgot how to hope.

Perhaps if we see each other again, Commodex . . . you can re-mind me.

In any case, the purpose of my message is this: I am about to set out on a mission and I may not return. If I do not survive, my wish is to be buried on Naboo, in the traditional way—and I would of course be honored if you would tend to me in death, and make sure that the people see me as they may have thought of me during my reign: peaceful, good, and fair. Strong.

And never, ever giving up hope.

And, Commodex, there's one more thing: I have kept this a secret from nearly everyone, and I hope you will be discreet. I am with child. And if I do not survive . . . that child must be kept safe. Please, sir: Do everything in your power to make it so.

I thank you for your many years of service, and hope that we see each other again, whether it is in this world or the next.

APHRA (narration):
Whoa. Okay. So the "good" queen sent Tahn his own special pen-pal letter right before she died. Her voice, I noticed, had the same terror I'd seen on my mother's face.

Padmé Amidala left behind loved ones, too.

And . . . hmm.

I pressed the holo again to see what would happen. More pen-pal letters? But, no. The image shifted once more, another holo of the former queen during her funeral. This was a wider shot, mourners trailing behind her.

And . . . yeah. She definitely looked pregnant. I'd known that already, thanks to the widely circulated holos of her funeral.

But *this* was the piece Vader had been especially curious about.

This was the secret thing he'd told me, the bit of information he needed to know more about. And he'd thought Tahn was the one person in the whole galaxy who could elaborate.

I brushed my fingers along the holo one last time, but the image stayed the same. Amidala. The mourners. The funeral.

I couldn't help but notice . . . her face looked sad. *Hopelessly* sad.

See what being "good" gets you?

APHRA:
You had a good life, Commodex. But now it's *over.*

Tahn screams again from the other room—

COMMODEX TAHN:
Stop! *Please!* I can't . . .

Oh, my queen . . . please forgive me . . .

SCENE 27. INT. BALCONY. COMMODEX TAHN'S HOME. MOMENTS LATER.

APHRA (narration):
It sounded like Trip was wrapping up his work, so I headed back out to the balcony.

TRIPLE-ZERO:
I believe Mr. Tahn is feeling more talkative now, Mistress Aphra.

APHRA:
Good, because I have *plenty* to talk about.

Commodex Tahn: Amidala's hologram when she was buried made her appear like she was still pregnant. But you, Mr. Mortician, were one of the very, very few people who had any access to the body. You are perhaps the only living person who knows the truth.

APHRA (narration):
His head snapped up, and he gazed at me through torture-fogged eyes. That surprised him—the fact that *this* was the information I was after.

APHRA:

Senator Amidala had given birth to a son.

Right? She *wasn't* still pregnant when she died; she'd actually given birth, and the child lived. The Jedi took the boy and put him into hiding. This can all be over if you just confirm what we already know.

A weighted beat as Tahn struggles with this.

COMMODEX TAHN:

Y-yes. She had a *son.* A healthy boy. They took him away.

I don't know anything else.

Forgive me, my queen.

APHRA:

Triple-Zero? Finish up.

Triple-Zero sends deadly blasts of electricity coursing through Tahn's body. Tahn screams—one last time—in pain.

TRIPLE-ZERO:

Thank you for your cooperation.

Oh, I do love my work.

I have to say I don't entirely approve, mistress. I'm sure he could have told us a whole lot more. Some of it might have even been useful!

APHRA:

No, Triple-Zero. We were here to *do the job,* not be sadists.

TRIPLE-ZERO:

Hmhh. Kindly speak for yourself.

BEETEE:

BLEEEEEEEEP!

APHRA:

So, there's a possible Naboo heir out there. Vader'll be glad to know the full story.

APHRA (narration):

If that *was* the whole story. With Vader, one could never be too sure.

But . . . I was starting to piece together at least *part* of the story. I could start to see the full picture coalescing, the pieces of who Vader was—and what made him tick—coming into focus.

And it was a very interesting story indeed.

SCENE 28. EXT. UNIVERSITY OF BAR'LETH. DAY. FLASHBACK.

APHRA (narration):
Okay, okay—I know there's something I said before that you really, *really* want to come back to. I can just picture you staring at me all earnest-like, batting those long lashes . . .

"Chelli," you'd say, "that bit about you 'barely having feelings.' How can that be true? You've been through so much, you've survived so many cruel twists and turns of life!

"And you certainly still have plenty of *negative* feelings about everything from chatterplants to Utani Xane and Sava Toob-Nix treating you like the tiniest, most squashable little bug."

Sure, ya got me. But remember I said "barely." You'd call that qualifier a convenient out. I call it finding a door.

Same thing, different interpretations.

The truth is, there's been a time or two when I've let my softer feelings out.

It's always ended badly.

Take this sweet little moment I had with Sana, not long after we got together. It was a beautiful day, sun filtering through the trees and casting dancing light patterns over the picnic lunch we'd packed. We were sprawled out on one of the Bar'leth campus's grassy expanses. Relaxing.

She was playing with my hair. She's the only person I've ever *let* play with my hair. I think in part because she was always so stoic. Fiddling with someone's hair is, like . . . tender? It felt like a secret that was just for us. A little tiny window into the psyche of the unknowable Sana Starros.

I think she always prided herself on that "unknowable" bit. So I'm not sure why she wanted to know *me* better.

SANA STARROS:
Okay, so . . . Kalandra, Yoshi . . . who else are you seeing besides me?

APHRA:
Darlin', I told you. It's hard to keep track.

But I've been avoiding Kalandra since she started staking out my classes, waiting for me to emerge—such a stalker. Who needs *that*? And Yoshi came down with Wookiee flu right after we had our first . . . encounter. Blech, I can't be around that level of snot and vomit. It's *Wookiee*-level. Don't try to picture it, it's too gross.

SANA STARROS:
Wait a minute—are you saying . . . the only person you're seeing right now . . . is *me*? We're each other's only . . . people?

APHRA:
Ew. Keep talking like that and *I'm* going to vomit. Wookiee-level.

SANA STARROS:
Chelli . . .

APHRA:
Ugh, fine. What can I say, Sana Starros? 'Tis a very hard task to keep my interest. But I can't seem to stop being interested in you.

SANA STARROS:

Mmm. The . . . *interest* is mutual.

APHRA:

Awesome. Let's make out.

SANA STARROS:

Chelli! Come on, talking like this is nice. Tell me something about yourself. Something nobody else knows.

APHRA:

I have a weakness for Bar'lethian plum cookies?

SANA STARROS:

Everyone knows that. No one in this entire university would even think of getting between you and the last Bar'lethian plum cookie, come dinnertime . . .

APHRA:

Only because that one time I tripped that snotty third-year who thought he was *entitled* to it.

Okay. I told you something. *Now* can we make out?

SANA STARROS:

[chuckling]

Mmm. You make me laugh.

APHRA:

You're an easy laugh.

SANA STARROS:

I'm actually not. I . . . I don't let my guard down much. I know what they say about me: Studious Sana. Never cracks a smile, never misses a class. Always at the library, always buried in some ancient text. But I am having . . . feelings while I'm doing all that, you know?

APHRA:

Why don't you like to show all those feelings, then? Let people see the nonstudious side of you.

SANA STARROS:

I think it's because . . . hmm.

I have often been in situations where I don't feel . . . safe. I've learned I have to make *myself* safe—no one else will do it for me. And one way to make myself safe is not showing . . . any of that. Keeping it all inside.

APHRA:

[obviously affected by this but trying to deflect]

Ah. Well. I mean, I don't understand that at all. People always know what I'm feeling—I just let it *all* out. Open book.

SANA STARROS:

I don't think that is true. I think you understand not feeling safe, Chelli. I think you understand better than anyone.

APHRA:

I . . .

A weighted beat as Aphra wrestles with this.

APHRA:

[blurt]

My mom died on the backwater planet she carted me off to when I was a kid, I was cold and hungry and lonely all the time, and I never want to feel any of those things *ever again*.

SANA STARROS:

Oh, Chelli . . . but what about *good* feelings? What about love?

APHRA:

Love is a trap. I think my mom loved me *too* much. That's why she took me away. But her love didn't keep us safe. And it only meant that right before she died . . . she was terrified. She was *weak*.

I don't want that. Ever.

SANA STARROS:

Have you *ever* felt safe?

A weighted beat as they stare into each other's eyes, Aphra considering this. Then, finally . . .

APHRA:
Right now.

APHRA (narration):
And then we *finally* made out. I know—Studious Sana actually ended up being quite the chatterbox, eh? Blah, blah, blah, *feelings*.

But . . . that actually sounds nice, right? Like this whole toothachingly sweet moment ended with us doing a whole lot of kissing, so . . . wasn't letting some of my softer feelings out actually a good thing?

Well, no. Because this wasn't the end of our story. Far from it.

After that, we . . .

The recording goes fuzzy.

APHRA (narration):
Recording, delete that last bit. There are some things no one needs to know but me.

SCENE 29. INT. CAVE. ANTHAN PRIME.

APHRA (narration):
Back to the stuff that's actually interesting! I returned to the caves of Anthan Prime to rendezvous with Vader. As usual, that dark, impenetrable mask gave nothing away. But I was learning how to study him closely—where to look for his tells. The way his shoulders would stiffen or his gloved fist would clench—they were the tiniest of movements, but I saw them all.

I tried to relay everything I'd learned from Commodex Tahn without embellishing *too* much.

I did okay with that part, but I couldn't contain my growing curiosity—I knew Vader was trusting me more and more, but I needed him to divulge more of his secrets. I needed to figure out how to use his power for my own gains, my own epic quest.

So I worked in a little strategic prodding about some of the things I was starting to piece together . . .

APHRA:

That's my report. In short: Your sources were right. She had a son.

A weighted beat of Vader's breathing.

APHRA:

And I mean . . . this is our farm kid, right? Our Death-Star-destroying pilot, Skywalker? Is that why you were so curious about Amidala giving birth, Lord Vader?

DARTH VADER:

Did you discover anything else?

APHRA:

Nothing relevant, really. I mean, Tahn really loved her—Amidala. Sounds like she was something special.

APHRA (narration):

I . . . don't know why I said that part. Except that being around Vader and his inscrutable mask was still extremely intimidating, so sometimes I babbled to fill the space. But for some reason . . . that *particular* bit of babble seemed to hit him right in the gut. He went silent for a long moment, staring into the dark abyss of the cave. There was that ever-so-slight stiffening of posture. A little thrill ran up my spine. I'd hit on *something*.

Another bit of information to file away—why did *this* affect him so much?

And notice that he didn't *exactly* confirm my brilliant conclusion about the farm kid—but he didn't deny it, either. So I was pretty sure I was right.

While he was doing his broody thing . . . I also couldn't help but fixate on what I'd just said. Did *I* think Amidala was special? How could I? She'd been good and weak, in the exact same way that my mother was good and weak.

That wasn't special. That was *predictable*. That was something I never wanted to be.

Amidala, the good queen . . . she would never have looked for doors the way I did. And she *definitely* wouldn't have made her own.

So why could I suddenly not stop thinking about the deep love and care in Tahn's voice when he spoke of her, the way she'd been so desperate to hold on to *hope* . . .

I brushed the thought aside and refocused on Vader.

APHRA:

Er . . . anything else on the to-do list, Lord Vader?

DARTH VADER:

Another Imperial agent has been tasked to locate the boy who destroyed the Death Star. We must find him first.

APHRA:

The Ante was hinting he knows a lot. If Imperial Intelligence has a lead, I'll bet he'll have better.

DARTH VADER:

You have the funds. Arrange a meeting. Offer what is required.

APHRA:

On it. Any other problems on the horizon?

DARTH VADER:

I have a new adjutant, courtesy of the Emperor's current lack of . . . faith in my abilities. And said adjutant is . . . somewhat eager and enthusiastic.

APHRA:

Anything to worry about?

DARTH VADER:

I have no fears. He suspects nothing. But I will need you to handle the journey back to Anthan Prime and this meeting with this "Ante" person yourself while I assure my adjutant of my loyalty to the Empire.

APHRA:
You got it, Boss.

APHRA (narration):
"New adjutant," eh? I did *not* like the sound of that. I mean, here I was, giving it my all. Showing Vader that *I* was the best adjutant he could hope for—the one who was most definitely *not* going to use whatever weakness he revealed to her advantage. And the Emperor up and sticks him with some low-rent *babysitter* who mostly just seemed to be getting in his formidable way? And, even worse, could very possibly get in mine?

I'd just have to keep proving myself. Vader was clearly becoming increasingly aware of my brilliance—sending me on yet another solo mission was definite evidence of that.

He was *seeing* even more of me. And I was seeing more of him.

I'd just have to make sure this blasted babysitter didn't muck everything up.

SCENE 30. INT. GAMBLING PARLOR. THE SPIRE. ANTHAN PRIME.

APHRA (narration):
And so I returned to the glitter of the Spire, where the gaseous storms outside were putting on quite a show . . .

Atmosphere: The storms buffet the station, shaking it around.

APHRA:
Wow, The Ante. Those storms are *fierce*. You're not at all worried about having your base here?

THE ANTE:
They bring the tourists here to gaze at their splendor. That covers a lot of my business. They're safe as long as you're not foolish enough to actually try flying through one.

APHRA:
Why do you look right at me whenever you say the word *foolish*?

THE ANTE:
Why do you think?

In any case, it's a little like having localized asteroid belts, with considerably more style.

APHRA:
Can you navigate them?

THE ANTE:
As much as you can navigate an asteroid belt. As in, not reliably.

I'm a man who likes sure things, Aphra.

APHRA:
That's funny. I'm a woman who doesn't believe in sure things.

TRIPLE-ZERO:
And, if I may add, I'm a droid who likes holo-chess!

BEETEE:
BLEEP! BLEEP!

TRIPLE-ZERO:
As Is Beetee!

APHRA:
Here's some credits—go have fun, guys. The Ante and I can handle our business without you.

TRIPLE-ZERO:
Oh, Beetee! This is even more exciting than torturing organics . . .

BEETEE:
BLEEP! BLEEP BLEEP!

TRIPLE-ZERO:
No, no, very sage—*nothing's* more exciting than that!

APHRA (narration):
The Ante and I settled into his lair—him in his ridiculously ostentatious chair, me in a much less resplendent piece of furniture. I noticed my chair was just a hair shorter in the legs—classic negotiating technique. Put the other person at a *slightly* lower level so they feel like they have a constant disadvantage.

APHRA:

We need the location of a man, Luke Skywalker. He's the pilot who destroyed the Death—

THE ANTE:

I know who he is and why people would be looking for him. You're not the only one who's been trying to find this talented young man. There are other . . . interested parties. Demand has upped the price. Here, let me pull up my display of the most recent figure. It's been changing by the hour.

The Ante pulls up a series of numbers on a holodisplay.

APHRA:

Whoa. That *is* an exciting number. Who else have you sold to?

THE ANTE:

No one. That's why the price is so high.

APHRA:

And am I meant to believe that?

THE ANTE:

All crime lords are greedy. We want profits and power. We do not pursue this line of work out of altruism. However, most lack self-control. I do not. In the long run, a reliable trading partner will make more profit. Eventually someone will pay my price, and everyone will be better off.

Aphra slides an overflowing bag of credits across the floor to The Ante.

APHRA:

Glad to be that someone. Keep the change, eh?

THE ANTE:

You bring this much here? With nothing but a pair of droids for protection? You *are* trusting.

APHRA:

All crime lords are greedy, wanting profits, power, and plush cushions. But I understand that you, The Ante, do not lack self-control and blah blah blah, fancy prepared speech to recite while fronting during deals.

THE ANTE:
This is a rather *large* amount of Imperial credits. I had my suspicions about the Son-tuul Pride's fortune . . . I'd say this very circumstantial evidence would confirm my prejudices.

APHRA:
Can we stop with what I can only presume is crime lord flirting? No, I don't want to see your enormous undercover operation!

Give me the kid's location and let me get out of here.

THE ANTE:
He's on Vrogas Vas.

APHRA:
Vrogas Vas? Really?

THE ANTE:
I'd bet my life on it.

APHRA:
The Ante, you are the best.

SPIRE SECURITY (on comm):
Imperial raiders approaching! Alert! Alert!

APHRA:
Oh, great.

Aphra taps her comm.

APHRA:
Aphra to Triple-Zero: Get yourself and your little murder buddy back to the *Ark Angel*! We're about to get visitors.

TRIPLE-ZERO (on comm):
But mistress, I'm *winning*!

APHRA:
Now, Trip!

APHRA (narration):
Once again, it was time to run. Luckily, I'd already accomplished my mission for Vader—now I just had to stay alive long enough to tell him.

SCENE 31. INT. GAMBLING PARLOR. THE SPIRE. ANTHAN PRIME. MOMENTS LATER.

Atmosphere: The parlor has been overtaken by a massive firefight! Aphra runs through, dodging blasts . . .

APHRA:
[muttering as she dodges]

Okay, okay, you got this . . . remember how *excellent* you are at staying alive. Just keep dodging all those blasts. Dodge! *Dodge!*

Ugh, how did this . . . escalate so quickly?

And why do I have a feeling my dearest darling murder robots had something to do with it?

A particularly explosive blast nearly takes Aphra out.

APHRA:
Arrrgh! Okay, Chelli: Just keep running. Legs. Move. *Faster!*

APHRA (narration):
Yeah, so. My dearest darling murder robots totally had something to do with it. But more on that later. The whole gambling den was in chaos—dealers bleeding out on the floor, panicked patrons scrambling for the exits, stormtroopers shooting at everything in sight . . .

As I pumped my arms and legs, my heart rate ratcheted upward, the infernal organ beating so hard and so loud, I thought it was going to beat its way clean out of my chest.

Exhilaration roared through my blood, forcing me to move even faster.

I'd managed to gather the info the Dark Lord needed. I was one step closer to gaining all his trust and learning all his secrets.

Now I just had to get outta here.

All of a sudden, The Ante's voice rang out over the blasts . . .

THE ANTE:
That's her!

APHRA (narration):
Why did I turn and look? *Never look behind you.* That's one of my mottoes!

But The Ante's voice distracted me momentarily . . . probably because I knew—I just *knew*—he was pointing right at me.

Oh, The Ante—and here I thought we were friends, you scummy, double-crossing nerf herder!

When I spared that split-second glance in his direction, I got another very unpleasant surprise.

The person he was pointing me out to?

None other than Darth Vader. Accompanied by a fussy-looking man who appeared to be held up by a ramrod-straight spine and the misguided belief that he's always right.

Was this . . . the new adjutant? The *babysitter*? He wasn't impressive looking *at all*. I was pretty sure I could take him in a fight—all I'd have to do is wrinkle his perfectly pressed uniform and he'd *fall apart*.

Whatever Lord Vader was up to, clearly our secret connection needed to *stay* a secret. Especially from Mr. Uptight Pants over there.

So I kept running.

And, thanks to The Ante, the stormtroopers turned all of their shoot-'em-up attention to *me*.

APHRA:
Void. Okay . . . it's okay. Only a little ways to the *Ark Angel* . . . just get down the corridor that leads to the hangar, get through the blast door . . . and you're home free. Let's *go*.

Aphra runs toward her ship, stormtroopers in hot pursuit, shooting at her.

APHRA:
Aphra to Beetee! Shut the blast door in the approach corridor!

We hear the creaky sound of a blast door starting to lower.

APHRA:
Not that one! The one behind *me*! Oh, doesn't matter. I can make it . . . I can make it . . . I can make it . . .

Aphra slides beneath the closing blast door.

APHRA:
Made it.

Triple-Zero? I'm incoming. Get the engines running. I'll be with you in two—

The hangar doors open, and we hear the heavy breathing of Darth Vader.

APHRA:

[sotto]

Void.

[normal voice]

Hi, boss. This is tight, but I can get away. We have—

DARTH VADER:

Silence.

APHRA:

Lord Vader. Sir. I don't know what The Ante told you—

DARTH VADER:

He identified you as the person behind the Son-tuul Pride robbery—naturally, the Empire has been very curious about the culprit. And my new adjutant is very *dogged* when it comes to pursuing things the Empire is curious about.

APHRA:

Ugh, that guy looks like such a pinheaded, bureaucratic little jerk. He's not worthy of you, my lord—

DARTH VADER:

I said *silence.* I have taken great pains to keep you hidden, Aphra. And yet, you seem intent on making a scene and exposing yourself to those who wish to remove me from power. If my adjutant had learned more about you—

APHRA:

But he didn't! I . . . I never told anyone *anything.* The Ante has no clue who I'm working for. And as far as the, ah, *scene,* I can explain—

DARTH VADER:

I do not think so. The Ante *was* about to reveal a great deal more about you. I could not have that, so I directed a stray blaster shot his way.

APHRA:

Whew, that's great news, boss! Real quick thinking on your part. Only a brilliant mind like yours could come up with something like that on the spot—

DARTH VADER:

The Ante will trouble me no further . . . and neither will you.

APHRA:

Wha—

DARTH VADER:

Do not struggle.

Vader draws his lightsaber and raises a hand, Force-choking Aphra—lifting her off the ground.

APHRA:

Vader . . . my lord, *no.* I . . . I'm the one you trust, remember? I've been loyal, I've done so many things for you . . . things only I can do! I have *skills. Skills you* noticed! Skills you need! This *can't be* how it ends . . . this . . . can't . . . be . . .

She struggles, trying to breathe. Trying to speak. Trying to live.

APHRA:

Please . . . I know . . . where the boy . . . is . . .

Vader releases his hold on Aphra. She falls to the ground in a heap, breathing hard.

DARTH VADER:

Tell me.

APHRA:

I will . . . *later.*

APHRA (narration):

I barely got those words out—I still can't believe I said them at all. I was still struggling to breathe after feeling Vader's invisible hand around my neck.

Air rushed back into my lungs, the hard, unforgiving metal of the hangar floor scraping against my knees. A good kind of pain—the kind that reminded me I was still *alive*.

Vader turned his back to me and sheathed his lightsaber. For the first time, I wondered what it would feel like when it touched my skin, blazed through bone and sinew, taking my life in an instant.

I'd thought . . . that was what I wanted.

But for those few seconds where I couldn't breathe, where my vision started to blur and go black . . .

I realized that *any* method of death would always have those terrifying last breaths. That moment where you *know* you're going to die.

I thought of my mother, of Amidala. They'd both known. They'd both devolved into fear.

And for the first time . . . my exciting, action-packed new job didn't seem quite so exciting anymore.

Because I knew my face just now, when Vader had tried to choke the life out of me . . . it had that same fear.

I was *weak*.

Vader turned from me, studying the hangar.

APHRA:
I—

DARTH VADER:
Silence. You will answer for this.

APHRA (narration):
He raised a hand again and brought down the entire hangar ceiling. He was on one side of the resulting avalanche—and me and my ship were on the other. I heard the muffled sounds of him greeting the stormtroopers and his new adjutant. Telling them I'd prepared "a trap."

I wasted no more time. Even though the wind had been knocked out of me, I scrambled to my feet and got myself onto my ship.

This time, Vader had given me my door. I'd pretty much forced him to.

And I knew he'd make me pay for that.

SCENE 32. INT. THE *ARK ANGEL*. MOMENTS LATER.

APHRA (narration):
Despite being pursued by an Imperial cruiser and a whole mess of TIE fighters, we managed to pilot our way through the Spire's gaseous storm—the one The Ante thought was so attractive . . .

APHRA:
You know, I think The Ante was right—these storms really *are* pretty!

TRIPLE-ZERO:
I would concur, assuming you meant "pretty likely to kill you."

BEETEE:
BLEEP!

TRIPLE-ZERO:
I have to agree, Beetee, being terminated would curtail our future plans for havoc. Can we make speed, Mistress Aphra?

APHRA:
Almost through. Almost . . .

APHRA (narration):

I maneuvered us around a cluster of lightning bolts, their brilliant flashes of light bouncing off the *Ark Angel* and casting a sinister glow over the controls of my ship. Trip actually did look like he was plated in the most precious of metals for a second—just like he always wanted.

And then, suddenly . . . the Imperial blockade was all around us, the massive underside of the cruiser looming over the *Ark Angel.* I thought we were *done.*

But just as quickly as they'd shown up . . . they retreated. Vanished. Like there was some kind of divine intervention.

I'm pretty sure it was more like . . . Darth-Vader-style intervention.

But whatever, I'd take it.

TRIPLE-ZERO:

They're leaving.

BEETEE:

BLEEP!

TRIPLE-ZERO:

No, Beetee, I don't think *retreating* is the right word.

APHRA (narration):

I slumped back in my seat, the tension I'd been holding in every cell of my body evaporating.

APHRA:

I'm going to live.

TRIPLE-ZERO:

For now, Mistress Aphra.

APHRA:

[with a little less bravado than usual]

Spoilsport. Trip . . . what happened back there? Did you and Beetee somehow *start* that firefight?

BEETEE:

BLEEP! BLEEP BLEEP!

TRIPLE-ZERO:

Oh, Beetee is ever so pleased you noticed, Mistress Aphra! Indeed—we started the whole thing!

APHRA:

Okay . . . how?

TRIPLE-ZERO:

Well, mistress, as I mentioned when you called, I was winning quite handily at holo-chess—

BEETEE:

BLEEEEEEEP!

TRIPLE-ZERO:

Hmph, all right, Beetee, I don't know why you're suddenly such a stickler for accuracy! I suppose technically . . . I lost. Quite badly. But only because the dealer was such an awful cheater!

BEETEE:

BLEEP BLEEP!

TRIPLE-ZERO:

He did call me a sore loser, didn't he? Hmph. So, like a good sports-droid, I offered to shake his hand—

APHRA:

I can see where this is going.

TRIPLE-ZERO:

And then *you* called, mistress, and the Imperials showed up, but I was still feeling most distressed over what a terrible cheater that dealer was! So Beetee sent a cannon blast his way and—

APHRA:

And the Imperials thought you were shooting at them, so they opened fire, and the whole thing turned into a gigantic, flaming disaster.

TRIPLE-ZERO:
[deflated]

Well . . . yes, Mistress Aphra. You do know how to ruin the climax of a dramatic story!

BEETEE:
BLEEP.

TRIPLE-ZERO:
Beetee and I noticed Master Vader and his adjutant conversing with The Ante. And I may have . . . overheard a bit of your rather scintillating conversation with Master Vader over the comm. Is everything all right between the two of you?

APHRA:
You . . . overheard our conversation. And you just told me I'm going to live "for now." So. I think you already know.

TRIPLE-ZERO:
Just trying to be polite, mistress.

APHRA:
[deflating, exhausted]

Yeah. Why don't you guys go be polite . . . somewhere else?

TRIPLE-ZERO:
As you wish, mistress. Would a friendly handshake make you feel better?

APHRA:
Triple-Zero, please leave. Now.

APHRA (narration):
As I slumped further into my seat and the *Ark Angel* hurtled away from the flashing lights of the storm, I tried to ignore the tight knot forming in my chest.

But it just kept getting tighter.

I'd talked a big game to Vader about my lifestyle, how I knew I was lucky to be alive. How the longer I worked for him, the more likely I was to get a lightsaber through the neck.

How I'd claimed I didn't care, as long as it was quick.

But there was a truth I kept coming back to as my mother's anguished face flashed before my eyes . . .

Yes, Chelli Lona Aphra—rogue archaeologist, proud daredevil, secret attaché to Darth Vader—loved taking the kind of risks that meant she was more likely to die before her time was up.

But after feeling the Dark Lord's grip tighten around my neck, the breath start to leach from my body, I couldn't help but think . . .

Maybe she'd rather not.

And . . . there was something else. Something I was trying extra hard not to think about.

But as the knot in my chest tightened and tightened, making me feel as if Vader was stealing the breath from my body all over again . . . I couldn't stop going back to the moment when he'd ordered me to be silent. To not struggle. To accept my fate.

The way the soulless pits of his mask had looked right through me—unflinching, uncaring . . . he didn't even have to think twice about killing me. I was . . . a cog. A *thing*. A disposable bug to be squashed once I no longer served him.

I thought Vader truly *saw* me.

And I guess . . . I guess I thought if he were going to kill me, lightsaber or no, it would have been after an epic betrayal. Not because I'd made a tiny little *bungle*.

But no, he'd been more than ready to kill me over that bungle, no matter how tiny.

All he saw was another bit of trash to be thrown away and never thought of again.

To him, I was like dust on a chatterplant.

And he would have tossed me away—if I hadn't withheld a bit of information he desperately wanted.

I suppose I was foolish to even entertain the idea that I could matter to someone like that. And I don't know why the realization that I didn't . . . *bothered* me so much. I mean, I guess the easiest answer was because gaining his trust and impressing him so much—as I thought I'd been doing—made him easier to manipulate. And who's impressed by an inconsequential bug? Who even *thinks* about that bug? Who . . .

Aphra's voice catches as she gets a bit emotional. She quickly composes herself.

APHRA (narration):
I needed to . . . *strategize* about some aspects of my relationship with the Dark Lord.

It was like Sana said all those years ago: I had to make myself safe.

And I was the only person I could count on for that.

SCENE 33. INT. CAVE. ANTHAN MOON. LATER.

Atmosphere: Maybe we can hear those mysterious cave winds again to set the scene . . .

APHRA (narration):

Regrouping from my little . . . setback wasn't the easiest thing in the galaxy, but I did it. Once we'd escaped the Imps and the storms, I waited for Vader to contact me. I knew he would.

When the Dark Lord finally got in touch, he ordered me to meet him in another cave on another Anthan moon.

For once, I wasn't really looking forward to seeing him. I knew he wanted the information I had more than anything in the entire galaxy—that's why I'd instinctively known *that* was the thing to bait him with.

And when he sent me a time and place to meet . . . well, yeah, I considered running.

But ultimately I knew: That wasn't the thing that was gonna keep me safe.

Maybe *this* would show him how loyal I was. Maybe *now* he'd truly see me—and how valuable I could be. Maybe I'd finally be able to find those cracks in his armor.

And whenever fear skittered up my spine, I reminded myself: This is what you do. You *survive.*

TRIPLE-ZERO:
Mistress Aphra, I must question your wisdom in coming here. If I'm not very much mistaken, manipulating Master Vader by withholding information is the sort of behavior one would classify as "blackmailing him."

He was quite clear on what would result.

Though it does make a droid wonder *how* exactly he'll terminate you.

BEETEE:
BLEEP!

TRIPLE-ZERO:
Yes, Beetee, he certainly could do that.

BEETEE:
BLEEP BLEEP!

TRIPLE-ZERO:
Or that.

APHRA:
Guys. Not helping. Not helping at all.

DARTH VADER:
Well?

APHRA:
Aaaaah!

APHRA (narration):
You'd think his . . . unique style of breathing would make it impossible for Darth Vader to sneak up on people. And yet . . .

I didn't waste any more breaths trying to withhold or showboat my major info reveal. I just did it.

APHRA:

Vrogas Vas. The boy's on Vrogas Vas.

DARTH VADER:

I am surprised to see you here, Aphra.

APHRA:

I send you a message and run, and you'd hunt me down and kill me. I figure the only chance of me surviving is showing that I'm trustworthy.

I *want* to work for you. I've shown you what I can do. I can't do anything for you when I'm dead.

You'll keep me alive.

Hopefully.

DARTH VADER:

The past few days have given me an appreciation for your talent.

Do not make me regret this.

APHRA:

You know, one of these days, I hope we're going to get past this is-he-going-to-murder-me-this-time stage of our relationship.

DARTH VADER:

Hmm. Vrogas Vas. A pointless rock. Why?

APHRA:

No idea. Apparently there's some old Jedi temple there. Maybe he's sightseeing?

DARTH VADER:

There is no known temple there. If this is some manner of trick, I will know who is responsible. And you were correct . . . I *would* find you.

APHRA:
Un . . . understood.

APHRA (narration):
Yessss, back in the game, Chelli! See what happens when you take initiative and keep your eyes on the prize instead of moping around with your *feelings*? I *knew* you could do it.

Okay, fine: I totally *didn't* know that.

But I sensed I'd *really* impressed him this time.

And I was still piecing together all the information I'd gathered into something more solid. The picture was hazy . . . but it was there.

There was so much more to his interest in this kid than he was letting on. It was that *very slight* change in body language I'd noticed— that barely perceptible stiffening of shoulders that happened the first time I heard him say the name *Skywalker* . . . the fact that he hadn't killed me simply because I knew where the boy was . . . the stuff he'd muttered to himself on Tatooine . . . it all added up to an obsession that went way beyond professional.

That kid was the key to unlocking everything about Darth Vader.

And if I could find out why . . . well, maybe *that* was the key to making myself safe—and to finding my endgame.

Whatever it was I was supposed to get out of this epic quest.

SCENE 34. INT. THE *ARK ANGEL*.

APHRA (narration):
Of course everything ended up going horribly wrong. While I stayed in range on the *Ark Angel*, Vader used his own ship to enter the space above Vrogas Vas. I tried to give him a little extra intel on his destination . . .

APHRA:
Vrogas Vas is a barren world with no known native life-forms. Though more than its share of gaseous surface emissions. Sounds like our target found himself a lovely little place to hide.

DARTH VADER (on comm):
The boy cannot hide from destiny. Or from *me*.

APHRA:
Skywalker's on Vrogas Vas all right. The Ante was quite certain of it. Said he'd bet his life on it.

DARTH VADER (on comm):
The Ante no longer has a life with which to wager.

APHRA:

Then I guess I'm betting my life on it. You'll find your rebel there, Lord Vader.

DARTH VADER (on comm):

I had better, Doctor Aphra. Coming out of hyperspace now.

APHRA (narration):

Unfortunately, a nasty surprise awaited the Dark Lord . . .

DARTH VADER (on comm):

They were on maneuvers. They weren't expecting me.

APHRA:

What? *Who* wasn't expecting you?

DARTH VADER (on comm):

The three squadrons of rebel starfighters I see before me. If this was a trap, Aphra, you had—*kzzzt*—hope it kills me.

APHRA:

A trap? Vader, I would never . . . I wouldn't cross you! I may love danger, but I've never been big on *suicide*. But three squadrons? That's *dozens* of fighters. You've gotta get outta there!

DARTH VADER (on comm):

Your information was—*zzzrrk*—correct. Skywalker is here. I can sense him.

APHRA:

Never mind Skywalker! You've got to *run*!

DARTH VADER (on comm):

I am a *Lord of the Sith*. They are the ones who should be running.

APHRA:

Vader, can you hear me? *Vader?*

Vader's comm signal fizzles out.

APHRA (narration):

Well. This was officially *not good.*

I waited for Vader to reestablish contact. I waited for *hours*—nearly a whole day. Annnnnd nothing. So it was up to me to devise a plan. Taking initiative once again!

APHRA:
All right, Trip, Beetee: I've intercepted rebel communications that say Vader was definitely shot down over Vrogas Vas. No word yet if he's dead or alive.

At this point . . . I'm not sure which would be worse. But either way, we've got to go after him.

And if he's dead . . . well . . .

TRIPLE-ZERO:
Might I make a suggestion? We could always simply *murder* everyone we encounter. No matter the problem, I usually find that to be the most elegant solution.

BEETEE:
BLEEP!

TRIPLE-ZERO:
Beetee rather excitedly agrees.

APHRA:
We're flying into a nest of rebel troops, Triple-Zero. I expect you'll get your wish.

TRIPLE-ZERO:
How splendid. Did you hear that, Beetee? We get to torture and exterminate indiscriminately!

BEETEE:
BLEEP! BLEEP!

TRIPLE-ZERO:
Oh, I have a simply *delightful* feeling about this mission.

APHRA (narration):
I tried not to . . . *linger* on the question of what Vader would do if he decided I'd sent him into a trap on purpose. I mean, the answer

was always going to be something really bad, I knew that now more than ever.

I shook off the shiver that kept running up my spine and firmly reminded myself that I'd escaped his chokey hand once. And I was figuring out how I could use the information I was piecing together about Skywalker . . . strategically.

But for now, I threw my energy into devising yet another brilliant plan.

First, I called in reinforcements.

APHRA:
Hey, Santy! Long time, no talk.

BLACK KRRSANTAN (on comm):
RAAAAAAWR!

APHRA:
I know, I know—I'm sorry I haven't called. I am still very dedicated to helping you with your problem, but work's been *so busy.* Just waiting for the weekend, you know how it is!

BLACK KRRSANTAN (on comm):
GRAAAAARGH!

APHRA:
Never mind that, I need you on Vrogas Vas.

BLACK KRRSANTAN (on comm):
RRRRROOOOOWWWR?

APHRA:
Yeah, exactly! I'm sending you all the intel now. Get everything and *scramble.* Yes, that means I'll owe you. Yes, that "owe" means money.

BLACK KRRSANTAN (on comm):
GROOOWWWR!

APHRA:
Just . . . get your fuzzy behind out here! Aphra out.

TRIPLE-ZERO:

Oh, excellent! Company! Shall I prepare a selection of weapons? We *must* be good hosts.

APHRA:

Not yet, Trip. He'll be here soon enough, and he's got plenty of weapons—mostly his fists. Give me some visuals.

TRIPLE-ZERO:

Here's the holo, mistress.

APHRA:

What a scruffy-looking group. Honestly, I thought they'd be more impressive.

Give me the who's who.

TRIPLE-ZERO:

Luke Skywalker. The target. Destroyer of the Death Star, the reason why Master Vader is here. From our best sources, on his journey from dusty Tatooine to Yavin 4, he's garnered a few associates.

Leia Organa, princess. Survivor of Alderaan.

Han Solo, not solo, now in a team. Some manner of smuggler. Various bounties.

Oh—an R2 unit and a protocol droid. Collaborating scum, mistress. Rest assured, we'll show no mercy.

BEETEE:

BLEEP!

TRIPLE-ZERO:

Yes, I know, we *never* show any mercy. That's not the point, Beetee!

APHRA:

Han Solo. *The* Han Solo. Oh me, oh my. What *are* we going to do facing *Han Solo*?

TRIPLE-ZERO:

Is he particularly fearsome, mistress?

APHRA:

No idea, never heard of him. Guess I was hoping they'd at least look the part. Solo looks more like a guy in a bar who skips the tab rather than a hero of the Rebellion.

Okay, let's move. Triangulate the possible crash positions.

We've got a Dark Lord of the Sith to save.

TRIPLE-ZERO:

Before he escapes by himself, thinking you sent him into a trap, mistress?

APHRA:

Yes. That. The rebel army I can deal with.

Darth Vader is a whole lot scarier.

SCENE 35. EXT. VROGAS VAS. LATER.

APHRA (narration):
Vrogas Vas was just as dusty and barren as promised. But hey, after fighting our way through the undeniably beautiful, undeniably deadly storms of the Anthan Spire . . . a little dust seemed down-right refreshing.

I'd triangulated the possible crash positions—unfortunately, there were many, so I put one of my ship's computers to work, running an algorithm I'd built from scratch to narrow it down.

I'd tell you how it works, but I think you'd get lost pretty fast.

Then, finally—I had a stroke of *genius*.

Find Darth Vader and I still had to deal with the fact that he might think I'd knowingly sent him into a trap. But find the thing he was obsessed with, and . . . well, I could *guarantee* he'd be happy to see me. And maybe be reminded of both my genius and my loyalty.

So I ran the algorithm *backwards* (would try to explain that, would also confuse you) in an attempt to locate the *least* likely crash sites.

And one of those was the abandoned Jedi temple.

That's where we found Skywalker.

APHRA:
Okay, let's see if I can get him in sight on the binocs . . . and . . . *there*. I see him—there's Skywalker. And *there's* our way back into Vader's good graces. I gotta say . . . out of the lot of those unimpressive rebels, he's perhaps the *most* unimpressive.

TRIPLE-ZERO:
How do you mean, Mistress Aphra? I find most organics equally unimpressive.

APHRA:
He looks exactly like what he is: a fresh-faced farm kid who has no business putting himself in the line of an Imperial firing squad. But if he's what Vader wants . . . well, he's our prize.

TRIPLE-ZERO:
Then I believe it's time to go human hunting! That *will* be a treat. Humans are, in my experience, one of the *finest* game specimens.

APHRA:
No, forget the Death Star—even if the kid *looks* unimpressive, he still has some magic Force thing going on. And he went one-on-one with Boba Fett and came out on top—

TRIPLE-ZERO:
And these are deterrents? You have not seemed overly impressed with Boba Fett in the past—

APHRA:
Yeah, yeah, I know, but everyone keeps talking about what a fearsome bounty hunter he is, and we have to play this just right. That means taking . . . precautions. Which is *not* something I'm used to.

We can't use deadly force, and anything short of breaking out the heavy weapons and we're risking getting hit in the guts with his big space-stabber. Lemme focus my binocs . . . annnnd he's not alone . . .

TRIPLE-ZERO:

Is the traitorous protocol droid by his side? Hmmm, who to kill first . . .

APHRA:

No. I mean, he's with a droid, but not that one—it's the little R2 unit.

TRIPLE-ZERO:

Also a traitor.

APHRA:

Hmm. Idea!

TRIPLE-ZERO:

We could just kill Skywalker, Mistress Aphra. In my experience, most organics are pretty much interchangeable. Bring Lord Vader a couple more yellow-haired ones to make up for the loss. He'll get over it.

APHRA:

That won't be necessary. Come here, Triple-Zero—you're about to play the leading role in my latest and greatest master plan.

SCENE 36. EXT. VROGAS VAS. ABANDONED JEDI TEMPLE. LATER.

R2-D2:
BLEEP!

LUKE SKYWALKER:
[occasionally in unmarked conversation with R2]

Yeah, it *is* a strange place, Artoo. Looks like some kind of temple. Wait—this writing. I think this was written with a lightsaber. This was a *Jedi* temple.

I can feel it.

I . . . Ben?

And . . . someone *with* Ben?

My father—I sense my father. He's . . . his presence is so *strong* . . .

R2-D2:
BLEEP!

LUKE SKYWALKER:
No, Artoo. If I can concentrate, I can feel it.

APHRA:

Showtime, Trip. Remember, you have to sound all sweet and innocent. Helpful. Not like *you*.

TRIPLE-ZERO:

I am most capable of this, Mistress Aphra, I can assure you. But might I say, this gold paint is very . . . itchy.

APHRA:

You don't itch, Trip. And weren't you just telling me that you wanted to be plated in precious metal?

TRIPLE-ZERO:

A coating of cheap paint is hardly the same, mistress—

APHRA:

Trip. As our big boss would say, my patience is wearing thin. Be a team player, will ya? Now lemme hear that voice . . .

TRIPLE-ZERO:

This is most humiliating, mistress, to have to stoop to the level of such a cowardly traitor.

But very well . . .

We hear something like a shifting gear or a series of beeps/whirs/clanks as Trip switches his vocal processor over . . .

TRIPLE-ZERO:

[way too high-pitched]

I am C-3PO, revolting, flesh-sack-adoring toadie . . . no, that's not right . . .

[way too low-pitched]

I am C-3PO, despicable stooge with a giant metal rod up his . . . no . . .

[regular voice]

Curses, who would have guessed such simpering tones were so difficult to emulate . . .

We hear another series of gear shifts . . .

TRIPLE-ZERO:
[correct C-3PO voice]

I am . . . C-3PO, a protocol droid fluent in over six million forms of communication . . . and debasing myself on a regular basis via doing the bidding of useless organics.

APHRA:
Close enough. *Go.*

APHRA (narration):
Triple-Zero moved closer to Skywalker—and I could swear I saw a change in his gait. It was definitely more . . . helpful. Somehow.

TRIPLE-ZERO:
Excuse me, master! Oh, *there* you are! We were all so worried, Master Luke!

LUKE SKYWALKER:
Threepio! It's good to see you!

R2-D2:
BLEEP! BLEEP BLEEP BLEEP BLEEP BLEEEEEP!

APHRA:
[sotto]

Ugh, shut up!

LUKE SKYWALKER:
Calm down, Artoo! It's just . . .

Triple-Zero touches Luke's shoulder, sending a massive electric shock through his system.

R2-D2:
BLEEP! BLEEP!

TRIPLE-ZERO:
Oh, be quiet, you astromech annoyance! You flesh-loving scum have made your bed. Now you're going to *die* in it!

APHRA:

Ugh, Trip. Leave the one-liners to me. Okay, Beetee, let's go grab the kid before Trip electrocutes everything in sight.

BEETEE:

BLEEP!

TRIPLE-ZERO:

Thank the Maker you're here, Beetee! Mistress, I've managed to render Skywalker unconscious—

APHRA:

I can see that—his little astromech is still upright, though, and . . . is it releasing some kind of gas?

R2-D2:

BLEEP!

TRIPLE-ZERO:

Yes, it's trying to defend its fallen master! Isn't that . . . oh, what's the proper adjective?

APHRA:

Brave? Cute? Heroically in denial of reality?

TRIPLE-ZERO:

Pathetic.

Isn't that just utterly pathetic? Beetee? Perhaps you'd like to show this R2 unit how a *proper* droid should behave.

APHRA:

Beetee, don't get too close! And let's not get distracted with another . . . like, droid firefight!

TRIPLE-ZERO:

Heavens, Mistress Aphra, the things you categorize as "distractions" are most fascinating. Beetee, you tell this impertinent R2—

BEETEE:

BLEEP BLEEP!

TRIPLE-ZERO:
Yes! Exactly that!

R2-D2:
TWEEP WWUURUU BWOOP!

BEETEE:
BLEEP!

R2-D2:
BEEDA TWEET BWOOP WOOBEEP

BEETEE:
BLEEP BLEEP

R2-D2:
BRIP WUDDA TWEET PWEEOOO BRRRRRP!

TRIPLE-ZERO:
My, what language! He certainly is a foulmouthed little astromech!
I wonder if he's capable of backing up such talk?

R2-D2:
BEEDOO THWWWWWRK

APHRA:
Oh gods, no! Little R2 unit, do *not* fire on Beetee, that's when the
cannons come out! I repeat—

*As R2-D2 fires on Beetee, Beetee arms his massive arsenal of weap-
ons and unleashes all of his firepower.*

BEETEE:
BLEEEEEEEEEEP

R2-D2:
BLORP! WWWEEEEAAAAAAAAAH!

TRIPLE-ZERO:
Look at Beetee go! Wanton destruction really brings out his playful
side, doesn't it?

It's always nice to see someone who's passionate about what they do. Speaking of which, I'm *tremendously* excited to begin draining all the blood from this one's flesh.

APHRA:
Leave Skywalker's blood where it's at, Triple-Zero. Vader wants him in one piece.

TRIPLE-ZERO:
Perhaps if I only took a *small* amount. Say a few liters or so . . .

APHRA:
Hmm. Could've sworn I heard a ship. Let's get this guy back to the *Ark Angel* and . . .

APHRA (narration):
Yeah, there was no "and." Because just as Triple-Zero hoisted the Skywalker kid over his shoulder and we started to traverse the barren desert once more . . . a very annoying voice called out from behind a large series of rock formations.

HAN SOLO:
That's far enough! Drop the kid or I drop you!

TRIPLE-ZERO:
It appears we're being ambushed. Perhaps I can drain *their* blood. Oh, I hope there are *a lot* of them.

APHRA:
Let me guess! Han Solo, the infamous smuggler!

HAN SOLO:
Yeah . . . ! You've . . . heard of me? I mean, of course you have . . .

APHRA:
Of course! As of about five minutes ago.

HAN SOLO:
That's right, Han Solo the infamous smuggler here, and you'd better let the kid go!

APHRA:

I'm starting to understand why you've got so many bounties on your head! You're not very good at this sort of thing, are you? If you were, you would've shot first and given warnings later!

HAN SOLO:

Hey! I—

APHRA:

[interrupts]

Now let me tell you who *I* am! I'm Doctor Aphra!

Something tells me you've probably heard of *me*!

HAN SOLO:

[sotto]

Ah, poodoo.

[not convincingly]

No! Never heard of you at all!

APHRA:

Nice try! Let's talk about your options here, Han.

Maybe you think you can get a few shots into me before I make cover or zero in on your hiding spot! You're wrong, but let's say it's your lucky day and you manage to take me out! Your friend is still dead before a single drop of my blood hits the ground!

[sotto, to Triple-Zero]

Trip: Take the rebel kid and back slowly toward the cave we passed.

[normal voice]

My droid here can route a fatal charge through his palms quicker than you can blink!

TRIPLE-ZERO:

That's *me*! Hello, Captain Solo! I'm quite looking forward to tor-turing you later!

APHRA:

So unless you want this kid shocked into oblivion, you need to put down the blaster and—

HAN SOLO:

I've got a question for you, Doc! How's your droid friend gonna shock my friend when he's got no arms?

APHRA:

No arms? What's he mean, no arms?

TRIPLE-ZERO:

Oh, I'm just remembering something that might prove relevant. There was one bit of information I failed to include in the briefing earlier. The smuggler Han Solo has a known associate. Or a pet, I'm not sure. It's a . . . *furry* creature of some sort . . .

What are they called again? A . . . a . . . *Wok-Wok*? No, that's not it. Oh, my head is such a muddle, all this talk of torture has made me quite—

APHRA:

A *Wookiee*?

TRIPLE-ZERO:

Yes! His name is Ch . . . Chew something. Chew . . . bacca?

CHEWBACCA:

RRRRRRWWWWWGGHHHHH!

APHRA (narration):

He came out of nowhere, a mountain of brown fur and teeth. While he wasn't as massive as Black Krrsantan . . . he did have the element of surprise on his side.

And he used it to rip one of Trip's arms clean off his body.

CHEWBACCA:

RAAAAAAAARRRRRRGHHHH!

TRIPLE-ZERO:

Oh, heavens! What have you *done,* you fur-brained amateur dismemberer? That was my *best* dissecting hand!

Let's see how you like it when someone pulls *your* arms off!

APHRA:
Solo! Are you seriously hiding out in the rocks while your Wookiee does all the work! Some prince of smugglers . . .

HAN SOLO:
And you shoulda stuck to stealing guns instead of my friends, Doc!

Han Solo and Aphra fire on each other.

APHRA (narration):
While the thoroughly unimpressive Han Solo and I got acquainted, Triple-Zero set about making friends with Chewbacca.

CHEWBACCA:
ARRRRGGGHHHHH!

We hear a series of vicious whumps as Chewie wales on Triple-Zero with his dismembered droid arm.

TRIPLE-ZERO:
Ow! Stop beating me with my own arm, you cretinous animal! Oh, the indignity!

I'm not sure why you've developed such a deep-seated dislike for protocol droids, but I believe you'll find that Triple-Zero is quite unlike any protocol droid you've ever encountered.

For example . . .

A syringe pops out of Triple-Zero's middle finger.

TRIPLE-ZERO:
Most protocol droids don't house five hundred milligrams of Mandalorian xenotox in their middle finger.

Triple-Zero sticks Chewbacca with the syringe.

CHEWBACCA:
[whimper]

Rar . . .

TRIPLE-ZERO:

What's the matter, Wookiee? Feeling a bit *tired,* are you? Well, I'm sure you've had a long day of pulling people's arms off. Why don't I help you lie down and relax for a bit?

APHRA (narration):

Yeah, Trip took down a whole Wookiee! Maybe *he* should try his luck in the fighting pits.

Meanwhile, I'd managed to find cover behind one of the rock formations close to the surface. I crouched, blaster at the ready, trying to suss out Solo's position. I could hear bits and pieces of him talking to himself as he sent volley after volley of blasterfire in my direction . . .

HAN SOLO:

Heh, Doctor Aphra. Thought she was supposed to be smart. What kind of *idiot* takes cover right underneath a hive of wasp-worms?

Get ready for a nasty surprise, Doc.

APHRA (narration):

Okay, I didn't totally hear the bit about the wasp-worms. But what Solo didn't know was *he'd* taken cover . . . under the only other hive in the area.

And we both shot at those hives *at the same time.*

APHRA:

Solo, you utter moron.

They shoot at the hives at the same time, unleashing two giant swarms of wasp-worms.

HAN SOLO:

Aaaaahhh! Get 'em off! Get 'em off!

APHRA:

Aaaaaahhhhh! Not wasp-worms! *Anything* but wasp-worms!

APHRA/HAN SOLO:

AAAHHHHHHHGGGGGGHHHHH!

APHRA (narration):

Neither of us could see what was happening, we were both just rushing toward each other, covered in the things. They swarmed my face, my hands—everywhere. Slithery little creatures that merely make you shiver and squirm at first . . . but once they start stinging . . . forget it.

And of course, since Solo and I were mostly focused on the very pressing business of getting them *off*, we ended up crashing into each other and passing out, while the wasp-worms continued stinging merrily away.

I wish I had one of my trademark witty bon mots to cap this part of the adventure off, but all I can say is:

Ow.

While I was passed out . . . well, apparently the chaos just kept going.

Trip got a little too cocky about besting a Wookiee and didn't notice Skywalker regaining consciousness—until Skywalker drew a lightsaber and chopped Trip's *other* arm off.

More *ow.*

My poor, beaten-up droids stumbled around until they found me—still passed out.

I woke up, all muzzy-headed and covered in wasp-worm stings. The rebels, my droids informed me, were headed back to their ship. I ordered Trip and Beetee to follow the rebels—we needed the Skywalker kid alive.

Otherwise, I knew I'd feel Vader's hand around my neck again.

And this time, he might not let go.

SCENE 37. INT. THE *ARK ANGEL*. LATER.

APHRA (narration):
Somehow, I made it back to the *Ark Angel,* muttering about how much I *hate* wasp-worms all the way.

I settled myself into my seat—wincing as the still-tender parts of my wasp-worm-stung body screamed in anguish. I drummed my fingers on the arm of my chair and forced myself to *think.*

What was the best next step? I hadn't secured Skywalker. My algorithm hadn't narrowed down the crash sites enough for me to find Vader—and even if it had, he was likely long gone by now.

What else could I *do*?

Information. It all comes back to *information.*

I pushed myself out of my seat—which was *ow* again, ugh, I really hate wasp-worms—and made my way over to the part of my comm that I used to intercept Imperial signals.

Skywalker . . . Skywalker . . . maybe if I could learn more about him . . . maybe that would be a starting point, at least.

I scanned all the transmissions I'd intercepted for any mention of the kid.

And I found something *very interesting.*

I knew others had been looking for the kid. Vader had mentioned it, and so had The Ante.

But I hadn't known exactly *who* was looking for him.

I vaguely remembered Vader saying it was someone who worked for the Imps—the transmissions confirmed that and gave me even more beautiful, beautiful information to work with.

And, what a coincidence, this someone had *just* touched down on Vrogas Vas as well . . .

APHRA:
Aphra to Triple-Zero! Did you find Skywalker?

TRIPLE-ZERO (on comm):
Indeed we have, Mistress Aphra. And all is well. Skywalker is about to be subdued by Imperial stormtroopers!

APHRA:
What? No! Those aren't Vader's troops! They're with his rival— his name is Karbin. He's some Mon Calamari Imperial cyborg . . . guy who's *also* tracking down Skywalker! He's the one Vader's been trying to . . . to beat on this quest for Skywalker. To foil!

TRIPLE-ZERO (on comm):
Oh my. You don't mean—

APHRA:
Don't let them take Skywalker! No matter what! Do you hear me?

TRIPLE-ZERO (on comm):
But, mistress, those are Imperial forces. How are we ever to—

APHRA:

Do *whatever* you have to do.

TRIPLE-ZERO (on comm):

Message received! Beetee, prepare to be *extremely* happy. But leave some for me to torture, you selfish little murder bucket!

APHRA (narration):

Oof. Here's where things got *really* chaotic. I used the transmissions I'd intercepted to track down *Karbin's* ship—much easier than Vader's illicit vessel. And . . . *Void.*

Sorry. Your old pal Aphra still gets kinda frustrated thinking about this. Because somehow Karbin's forces had gotten hold of the Sky-walker kid and were dragging his unconscious form aboard their ship. I never got a clear answer out of Triple-Zero and Beetee as to how they'd failed to capture the kid, but my guess is the droids got a little too excited when I gave them permission to go all-out with the explosions and totally forgot about their actual mission.

I frantically scouted the area around Karbin's ship, searching for my favorite Sith Lord, desperately hoping that he *really* needed my help right now.

I found him not far from the ship—he and the Mon Calamari cy-borg were duking it out in an epic lightsaber battle!

Aphra makes epic lightsaber noises.

APHRA (narration):

And hey, now I was back in range! I reached out to Vader on the comm—and tried to crush the Bar'lethian flea-maggots dancing through my stomach. I'd just have to hope that now, when the Dark Lord's back was against the wall . . . I'd finally be able to prove myself beyond all doubt.

APHRA:

Vader! Are you there? It's me! Karbin's guys are dragging the Sky-walker kid aboard a transport. If you want to do something you need to do it *fast.*

The sounds of an intense lightsaber battle waft through Aphra's comm.

DARTH VADER (on comm):
I am delayed by this fool.

APHRA:
Let me help! This is my "redeem myself for accidentally leading you into a trap" opportunity!

DARTH VADER (on comm):
Mmm. Very well. Listen carefully.

APHRA (narration):
His plan . . . oh god. I wanted to object. Every cell in my body *screamed* at me to say no, to *run*.

To make myself safe.

But . . . I knew this was my chance. My *only* chance. It was a big, juicy door—and I had to go through it.

Because if I did . . . maybe I'd be able to achieve what I'd wanted to achieve ever since our adventure together began. I'd finally really *prove* myself and forge my path to becoming Doctor Chelli Lona Aphra: Super Important Amazing and Extremely Rich Adventurer That Everyone Is Totally Afraid Of.

And I'd *never* have to worry about his hand around my neck again.

So . . .

Aphra's voice gets a little teary.

APHRA (narration):
Sorry . . . I'm sorry. Recording, pause. I'll come back to this later.

There is a slight pause in the recording. When Aphra returns, her voice sounds tough—like she's steeling herself.

APHRA (narration):
Okay. I know you're just dying to know what happened next—you were always so impatient—so here it is: I followed Vader's orders

and dutifully piloted the *Ark Angel* over a bridgelike rock formation—right where Vader was leading Karbin.

DARTH VADER (on comm):
There is no future for you, Karbin.

APHRA (narration):
Man. How does he always have the perfect zinger for every situation? The Dark Lord looked up to the sky . . . and Karbin followed his gaze . . .

We hear the deep rumble of the Ark Angel *descending onto the bridge/rock formation—and then a massive crash.*

APHRA (narration):
And . . . That's right. I set the *Ark Angel*—my big, beautiful, perfectly-modified-to-my-exact-specs baby—right down on that fool's *head.* Er, and the rest of his body, too.

We hear more of the crash as the rock formation crumbles.

APHRA:
Aaaaaaaghhhh! Ejectejecteject!

Another massive crash as the Ark Angel *explodes.*

APHRA (narration):
You know—I wasn't entirely certain that ejector seat button would actually *work.* I'd never had to use it before. It is perhaps the only part of the *Ark Angel* I *hadn't* modified.

But it did work, and that's how I found myself floating over Vader in my sad little captain's chair as my ship crumbled to dust and the Dark Lord finished Karbin off.

Annnnnd . . . that was it. No more ship for the great adventurer Chelli Lona Aphra.

I . . . I know I said earlier that I don't have soft feelings. But . . . I had something close to them for the *Ark Angel.* I'd modified my baby with droid parts, taken refuge in its walls when I was being chased by so many people who wanted me dead . . . and that glorious ship helped me escape every time.

The *Ark Angel* had been my door more than once. I . . . *loved* that ship.

But I guess that just goes to show how *desperate* I was. I needed Vader to trust me again. I needed to show him that I'd sacrifice *anything*—and that I'd do it without flinching.

And I'm still proud to say this: When the *Ark Angel* exploded around me, all of its beautiful pieces crumbling to dust . . . I only flinched a little.

I swallowed hard, shoving down the tears bubbling up, and listened to Vader's final exchange with Karbin over the comm.

DARTH VADER (on comm):
You are not the only one capable of deception, Karbin. You will delay me from the boy no longer.

KARBIN (on comm):
This . . . this isn't just revenge for the Death Star, is it? This is something else . . .

DARTH VADER (on comm):
You will never know.

Vader kills Karbin with a mighty swoop of his lightsaber.

APHRA:
Great show, boss—you just cost me my ship. Am I back in your good graces?

DARTH VADER (on comm):
All rests upon the boy.

APHRA:
Great. Can you give me a little more than that?

DARTH VADER (on comm):
Find him. That is your task.

APHRA:

Okay, but . . . help me out here, your lordliness. Give me a . . . a clue on how to proceed. I mean, haven't I done pretty well by you? Finding you a droid factory, building you an army, robbing the Empire, getting you all this info on the Skywalker kid, destroying my beloved ship . . . not to mention almost getting killed multiple times—

DARTH VADER (on comm):

There is no need to boast, Aphra—

APHRA:

Maybe I could get just a little bit more . . . *insight* from you about the kid—

DARTH VADER (on comm):

I have nothing to offer.

APHRA:

[getting frustrated]

I think you do.

DARTH VADER (on comm):

What does that mean?

APHRA:

Just . . . look, you obviously have a bigger connection to this kid than you're letting on. If you'd just *tell* me what it is, it would help me accomplish . . . whatever it is you need to accomplish.

I won't let you down, I promise! I . . . I'm the best at this. Whatever this weird attaché/associate/right-hand-woman job is. And I've *proved* I'm the best.

You can *trust* me. You really, really can.

So tell me. Who is Skywalker?

A weighted beat of Vader's breathing. Then . . .

DARTH VADER (on comm):

[barely suppressed rage]

I am Darth Vader. I have commanded *legions*. Annihilated entire systems. Reduced the most powerful to *husks*. And I will *not* be spoken to like this by an upstart mechanic with delusions of grandeur.

APHRA:
M-mechanic? Is that all you think I am . . . after all this . . . after . . .

DARTH VADER (on comm):
Silence. Find the boy, Aphra. And do not even think of *breathing* near me until you do.

SCENE 38. EXT. VROGAS VAS. LATER.

APHRA (narration):
[deflated]

Yeah, so. Totally didn't play that one right.

I managed to get myself out of the ejector seat and away from Vader.

I wasn't sure if *he* had access to a working ship at this point—having been through a crash landing of his own and all—but he didn't offer me a ride.

And I knew better than to ask.

I was just feeling so . . . *lost*. I mean, I'd sacrificed my ship for Vader, and he hadn't even blinked an eye. He didn't seem to care. The way he'd talked to me . . . his voice held the same *contempt* as when he'd almost killed me.

He didn't see me at all, and maybe he never would.

Unless . . . I could track down the Skywalker kid. That seemed to be all he cared about.

I flashed back to that last exchange with Karbin, how Karbin had deduced Vader's obsession was about more than the Death Star.

I needed to know *more*. And I probably should have known better than to ask Vader about it so baldly, I just thought . . . well, never mind what I thought.

For now, I needed a ship.

I trudged through the desert, resisting the urge to scratch my now swollen wasp-worm stings. My whole body prickled, like the wasp-worms were crawling all over my skin . . . ugh.

Maybe a ship could magically appear? Just this once?

That didn't happen—but the next best thing did. Instead of a ship, a massive pile of fur appeared on the horizon—and he was waving at me.

BLACK KRRSANTAN:
GRAAAARGH!

APHRA:
Santy! Wow, you are a sight for sore eyes! I mean that in a good way, to be clear. Please don't rip my arms off. Unless that will stop the wasp-worm stings from itching.

BLACK KRRSANTAN:
RAWWWWWR!

Black Krrsantan envelops Aphra in a bone-crunching hug.

APHRA:
Ow! Careful, I've been through a lot . . . aw, Santy. Good to see you, too.

TRIPLE-ZERO:
Oh, Mistress Aphra! There you are.

APHRA:

Trip, Beetee! You guys look better. Trip, how'd you get your arms back?

TRIPLE-ZERO:

Not important, Mistress Aphra! The more relevant information is this: Black Krrsantan did not manage to foil the rebels as you'd hoped when you called him for this mission. But he did . . . *delay* them.

BLACK KRRSANTAN:

RAAAWR!

APHRA:

[wheels turning]

Wait a minute—Solo and those other jerks. They're still here?

TRIPLE-ZERO:

Indeed, mistress, they have not yet departed the planet! But we don't know where the Skywalker organic has gotten to. I'm afraid Beetee and myself got a little too caught up in the excitement of battle!

BEETEE:

BLEEP BLEEP!

APHRA:

Hmm. I'm getting an idea—

TRIPLE-ZERO:

Oh, mistress, every time you say that, it ends *disastrously.*

APHRA:

Shh, Trip. My idea's forming . . . percolating . . . almost there . . .

Suddenly Karbin's ship crashes onto Vrogas Vas—Aphra and Co. can see it in the distance.

TRIPLE-ZERO:

Oh my! What a rude interruption of your idea percolation, Mistress Aphra.

APHRA:

No . . . no, it's perfect. That's Karbin's ship . . . which Skywalker was supposed to be *on* . . . and his friends are still here, looking for him . . .

[beat]

Okay, got it.

Santy, Trip, Beetee . . . do you guys know where the rebels' ship is parked?

BLACK KRRSANTAN:

RAAAAWRRGH!

APHRA:

Good, then let's move. My idea's *ready.*

SCENE 39. EXT. VROGAS VAS. LATER.

APHRA (narration):
Do you know how easy it is to plant a minefield of bombs? What am I saying, of course you don't! That's something *you* would *never* do.

Also, it's actually quite hard.

Luckily, *I* know how—so with a little help from my friends, I found the rebels' ship, made a few minor tweaks, did a little explosives setup, and soon I was starting to feel a bit like my old self.

By the time the rebels tried to return to their ship, I was waiting for them—and when I saw that Skywalker was with them, a thrill jolted through my entire body.

Okay, this was it! My plan was so totally going to work . . .

Han Solo, Chewbacca, Luke Skywalker, R2-D2, and C-3PO approach the Millennium Falcon.

HAN SOLO:

Luke! Are you a sight for sore eyes.

LUKE SKYWALKER:

Han!

CHEWBACCA:

RAAAGH!

C-3PO:

Master Luke, thank the stars! Now we can leave.

HAN SOLO:

Anyone on your tail, kid?

LUKE SKYWALKER:

No one. Must have lost them.

HAN SOLO:

You must have a guardian angel.

LUKE SKYWALKER:

The Force, Han.

HAN SOLO:

Enough of that. Chewie, let's get the *Falcon* patched up and get out of here.

CHEWBACCA:

RAAAWR!

HAN SOLO:

Hey, the *Falcon*'s already been patched up!

APHRA:

Observant, Solo. I have made some truly wondrous improvements to your garbage heap ship.

But if you were *really* observant, you'd realize you're standing in a field of micromines. In case your friends don't quite have your eyes, this is a trigger in my hand. You can probably guess what it's for.

Clue: *minefield.* Drop your weapons.

HAN SOLO:
What do you want, lady?

APHRA:
For Vader not to throw me into deep space, mainly.

[on comm]

Hey, Vader. Guess what I've got? I'll extract them in their ship, we'll rendezvous later.

LUKE SKYWALKER:
You're actually with Vader?

APHRA:
Skywalker! So nice to see you again. I was *hoping* your very enterprising friends had found you. Too bad they're not smart enough to keep you from getting into even more trouble.

HAN SOLO:
You really don't know anything, do you, Doctor Aphra?

APHRA:
Not true, I am a treasure trove of highly classified and top-secret information. The things I could tell you . . .

PRINCESS LEIA:
Really?

Leia comes out of nowhere and punches Aphra in the face, knocking her out.

HAN SOLO:
Leia! Where did you come from? And what are you—

PRINCESS LEIA:
Never mind that. She says she knows things. Let's get her aboard.

APHRA (narration):
That's Princess Leia Organa—and I'm ashamed to say she knocked

me out cold. In my defense, she came out of nowhere! Never thought I'd get punched in the face by actual royalty—but I'm sure you're not surprised.

This princess was about to be the biggest pain in my ass. And given everything I'd been through . . . that was really saying something.

SCENE 40. INT. *VOLT COBRA*. ABOUT TWO WEEKS LATER.

APHRA (narration):
I awoke in a cold, gray cell on a cold, gray ship—the *Volt Cobra*. My wrists were in binders, I had no idea where we were going, and I was *starving*. Also, I had a sinking sensation that Darth Vader really, really wasn't going to like the fact that I'd gotten captured . . . and hadn't even come close to nabbing the Skywalker kid.

Things were *not* looking good for my Feared, Powerful, and Disgustingly Rich Adventurer aspirations. Or for my Staying Alive aspirations. Or . . . for anything.

But as I was about to discover . . . this was the least of my worries.

Yes, I just described Darth Vader as "the least of my worries." But I'm sure you'll understand why.

Anyway, the rebels running the show tried to interrogate me. They spent a couple weeks on that—I think. Time ceases to have meaning when your daily landscape looks exactly the same every godsforsaken hour. I gave them *nothing*.

After a certain amorphous amount of time in the joint, I learned that I had to yell really loud whenever I wanted food. I was just about to get started with my daily yelling when the door slid open, casting a small sliver of light on the dingy metal of my cell.

And then *you* walked in.

SANA STARROS:
Aphra.

APHRA:
Sana? Sana Starros? I . . . I . . .

SANA STARROS:
How refreshing to see you speechless. I don't think that's something I've *ever* had the pleasure of witnessing.

APHRA:
I . . . wow. You look great.

APHRA (narration):
Ugh. I have to cringe remembering how . . . how *fumbling* I sounded. In my defense: You *did* look great, Sana. But I didn't make this recording just to tell you that.

I . . . I wanted to tell you . . . I . . . um . . . *Void.*

The recording goes fuzzy.

APHRA (narration):
[sounding like she's composing herself]

Recording: Delete that last bit. Now. Where was I?

Oh, right—you and the whole "looking great" thing.

You . . . *your* . . . ugh.

Y'know what, let's go back to pretending I'm not recording this for anyone in particular, otherwise this is feeling a little too . . .

[intimate!]

. . . something.

[clears her throat, gathers herself]

So. *Her* dark-brown skin was as glowing as it had been when we were at university together; that mane of glorious midnight tresses still gave her the look of royalty. And her eyes were as sharp and probing as ever, boring into me like she could see my soul.

She always could. She was the only one.

But there was so much about her now that was *different*. Her quiet studiousness had been replaced by something . . . harder. She was made of pure steel now. And I was probably the only one who could sense the flash of hurt—the *softness*—percolating underneath all the steel she was giving me.

Listen, I was at . . . let's call it a low moment. All my defenses were down. I couldn't stop the wave of *yearning* that rose up in my chest, just seeing her look at me like that again.

SANA STARROS:

I look great? *That's* what you say to me? I . . . can't really say the same for you. Still causing trouble, though—that never changes.

APHRA:

Sana, you have to get me out of here! What are you doing, anyway . . . are you with the Rebellion now? How is that even possible, I thought I heard you became a smuggler? But look, we can escape together—

SANA STARROS:

Oh no. I've fallen for that before—never again.

APHRA (narration):

Hmm, yeah. I probably should have known she'd still be mad, even after all these years. She *definitely* wasn't in the mood to help me.

So I'd have to help myself. As usual.

I surreptitiously felt along the edge of my binders. Hmm. Yes. I knew this kind of locking mechanism. I twisted my right hand around, trying to get my thumbnail to line up just . . . *so* . . .

APHRA:

Wow, so . . . what have you been up to? Anything cool? I always thought you were destined for big things—

SANA STARROS:

Sure, you did. That's why you left me without so much as a good-bye, right? 'Cause you wanted to see me do big things.

APHRA:

I was doing you a favor!

SANA STARROS:

Which taught me never to accept favors from anyone—

APHRA:

Hey, that *was* the favor!

SANA STARROS:

Then I'd say you've done me *way* too many favors over the years—

APHRA:

I was teaching you important life lessons—

SANA STARROS:

Why are you like this—

APHRA (narration):

I felt the telltale click as my thumb landed on the left side of the locking mechanism. I needed to angle it just . . . right . . . without totally breaking my wrist.

There's a click as Aphra frees her right hand from the binders.

SANA STARROS:

Wait, what are you . . . dammit, Aphra!

Security!

Princess Leia and a rebel security detail storm Aphra's cell.

PRINCESS LEIA:

What . . . She got out of her binders again! Grab her! She's going for the blaster . . . *look out!*

A blaster fires.

APHRA:

All right, pinheads! I'm the one holding the blaster now. Last chance to turn this ship around. Or I start putting holes in all your pretty little faces. Starting with *you*, Princess.

PRINCESS LEIA:

You're quite good at getting out of binders, Doctor Aphra. That's, what, the fourth pair you've escaped?

But you won't be getting off this ship quite so easily. Not unless you've got a lot more than a single blaster up your . . . *Whuugh!*

The ship is hit by an explosive blast and shakes violently.

PRINCESS LEIA:

Holding cell to bridge! What in the blazes is going—*aah!*

SANA STARROS:

Gravity's knocked out . . .

APHRA:

Yeah, *obviously.* Let me guess. You let that idiot Solo be your pilot.

Rebel Alliance. Hmph.

APHRA (narration):

We may have been floating, weightless—but I kept a firm grip on my blaster. And I was so focused on holding on to that one precious thing, the key to my escape, my *door* . . . that I didn't see Sana's arm coming down on the back of my neck.

APHRA:

I don't know how Vader hasn't already wiped you guys off the— *WUHH!*

APHRA (narration):

And to add insult to injury, that was the moment the gravity came back on.

Aphra goes down—just as the ship's gravity is restored.

APHRA:
Guuuuh . . .

SANA STARROS:
Learned that little move from a k'Jtari pirate. That just cost you *extra,* Princess.

PRINCESS LEIA:
Whatever you say, Sana—at least the gravity's back. What's happening? Who's shooting at us?

SANA STARROS:
Your rebel friends, I'm guessing. If they put so much as a scratch on my ship . . .

PRINCESS LEIA:
I know! It's gonna cost me extra! Why didn't you transmit the clearance codes I gave you?

SANA STARROS:
'Cause I was busy cleaning up your mess!

PRINCESS LEIA:
Does it still cost me extra if you get us all killed?

SANA STARROS:
No. But you *yelling* at me will definitely be on the bill. I sure hope your little doc here is worth all this.

PRINCESS LEIA:
Believe me, she is.

SCENE 41. INT. SUNSPOT PRISON.

Leia and Sana escort Aphra into the prison.

APHRA (narration):
Back in the binders again. Hmph. Turns out, Sana and the princess were taking me to Sunspot Prison, an orbital facility that was flooded with constant bright, blinding light from a nearby sun. It was like being under the hot floodlights of an interrogation room *all the time.*

Atmosphere: While this is a badass, high-security prison, there is also something undeniably sad about it—oppressive, forgotten. All that heat surrounding it. A sense of danger permeates the air—but not the fun kind of danger Aphra prefers. The day-to-day existence here is excruciating.

PRISON WARDEN:
Greetings, Princess. Welcome to Sunspot Prison. The biggest, baddest penitentiary the Alliance has to offer. May your stay here be a short one.

PRINCESS LEIA:

It will be, Warden. For all but one of us.

PRISON WARDEN:

As you can tell, we're a bit touchy about security. Can't risk the Empire finding out about this place. Most people in the Alliance don't even know it exists.

We've got war criminals. Imperial spies. Mercenaries. Even a moff or two.

Some prisons, the inmates complain about being locked in deep, dark dungeons where they never see the sun. That's one complaint we never get here.

Does tend to get a bit warm, but you get used to it. After a few years or so.

APHRA:

Trust me, I won't be here that long.

PRISON WARDEN:

They all say that. Doctor Aphra, is it? And what might your story be?

APHRA:

My story is I'm gonna burn this place to the ground. And you with it, Warden. That's if you're lucky. If you're *not* so lucky, my good friend Darth Vader might just pay you a personal visit.

PRISON WARDEN:

Let's hope he does. We've got room for him as well.

PRINCESS LEIA:

She's not lying about her connection to Vader. The Empire will be scouring the galaxy for her.

PRISON WARDEN:

Even if they could find us, which they can't, we're quite well defended here, Princess. We've got a star at our back and a sea of ion cannons in front of us. Believe me, as hard as it is to break out of this place . . . it would be just as impossible to break *in*.

Now, Doctor, let me show you to your cell.

Sana and Leia follow Aphra as guards lead her to her cell.

SANA STARROS:

Has Aphra said anything, Princess?

PRINCESS LEIA:

Other than elaborately gruesome threats and the most colorful insults I've ever heard? No.

She was questioned for weeks by Alliance Intelligence officers. She gave them *nothing*.

SANA STARROS:

I bet it was quite the interrogation. What'd they do, shine a bright light in her face? Play their music real loud?

The Empire wouldn't stop there.

PRINCESS LEIA:

Which is one of the reasons we're fighting a war against them, Sana.

SANA STARROS:

And one of the reasons you're going to *lose*.

PRINCESS LEIA:

Humanity isn't the same as weakness.

SANA STARROS:

When your life is on the line, it is.

PRINCESS LEIA:

I refuse to accept that.

SANA STARROS:

Tell that to a stormtrooper next time you see one, and see if he refuses to kill you.

PRINCESS LEIA:

I brought you on this trip, Sana, so we could move past the awkwardness of our initial meeting.

APHRA (narration):

Well, *that* totally made my ears perk up! Was there a . . . connection between the princess and Sana? I never would have pegged Sana as having a thing for princesses. Then again . . . after all the stuff I subjected her to, maybe she decided it would be better to go with someone who was the complete opposite of her usual type.

SANA STARROS:

And I came because you pay me well, Princess. And because you saved my life on Nar Shaddaa. Doesn't mean I have to agree with you.

PRINCESS LEIA:

Your right to disagree is one of the things we're fighting for.

SANA STARROS:

Yeah, well. That's one right nobody's ever been able to take away from me.

APHRA:

Wait, what? You know I can hear you, right? Are you guys just . . . debating politics now? Snooze, Sana, I expect better of you!

SANA STARROS:

Shut it, Aphra!

PRINCESS LEIA:

So what would you do with Doctor Aphra, if you were in my shoes?

SANA STARROS:

I'd *make* her talk.

PRINCESS LEIA:

And if you couldn't, no matter what you tried?

SANA STARROS:

Then I'd toss her into the star and be done with it. Only way to ever be sure she won't someday come back and kill you.

Because believe me, a woman like *her* . . . that's *exactly* what she'll do.

APHRA:

This is character assassination, Sana! Darth Vader isn't gonna like you talking about his favorite associate like that!

SANA STARROS:

Do I look like I care?

The warden locks Aphra in her cell.

PRINCESS LEIA:

You start to feel talkative, Doctor, have the warden give me a call. Until then . . . enjoy the sunshine.

APHRA:

Am I really supposed to be afraid of a little sunlight? They know I work for Darth Vader, right?

SANA STARROS:

Don't look at me. I told them to kill you.

APHRA:

Yeah, I just bet you did, Sana. Hey, I've got a better idea. How about you get me outta here?

SANA STARROS:

And why would I wanna do that, Doc?

APHRA:

I don't know, for old times' sake?

SANA STARROS:

Nice try. But our old times were never all that great.

APHRA:

Same old Sana. You always drive a hard bargain. Fine, just name your price.

APHRA (narration):

Sana went quiet then. The princess just cocked an eyebrow and wandered off—like, *You deal with it.*

I was hoping Sana would turn, face me, let me plead my case. I always knew how to make big, pleading boggling eyes at her—I'm proud to say I had it down to a *science*. And she was always a sucker for that look.

But she didn't turn around. And she stayed silent.

I . . . hadn't really had time to worry since I'd been kidnapped by the rebels. I mean, worrying isn't something I generally do anyway, but I'd been so focused on getting out of those binders . . . on escaping . . . on finding my door . . . The adrenaline rush had powered me through.

Now I was stuck in a cell that was getting hotter by the second, the tiny slit of a window near the ceiling welcoming the relentless blaze of the sun.

Sweat pricked my brow. And that wormy feeling that was so foreign to me—*worry*—percolated in my gut.

And Sana still wasn't saying a word.

APHRA:
Sana?

SANA STARROS:
How about you just tell these people what they want to know, Aphra? Wouldn't that be a lot easier?

APHRA:
What? Are you kidding me? Don't tell me you're . . . Sana Starros, rebel sympathizer. I never thought I'd live to see the day.

SANA STARROS:
Yeah, well, don't worry. By the looks of this place, you *won't*. See ya around, Doc.

APHRA:
Smugglers. I hate smugglers.

APHRA (narration):
I'd wanted to say something with bravado. Something that would get her to turn around. And she did turn for just a moment . . .

There was that *hurt* flashing through her eyes again.

Maybe it's because I was at such a low moment—captured by the rebels, no idea what Vader had planned for me, no doors in sight . . . but it got to me.

I knew I was the one who'd made the glorious Sana Starros *hurt* that way.

I slumped to the ground of my cell. And even though I tried like mad to block it out . . . the memory of the moment I left her flooded my mind—like the sun flooding my cell.

Constant, all-consuming, refusing to be ignored.

SCENE 42. INT. APHRA'S DORM ROOM. UNIVERSITY OF BAR'LETH. DAY. FLASHBACK.

APHRA (narration):
This part is . . . well, I guess it *should* be embarrassing. Even more embarrassing than all the other stuff I've told you.

But that's the thing: I'm not embarrassed by this part at all.

I still believe I did the right thing.

It was just a few weeks before graduation day. We were lazing around together in my dorm room . . . it's so weird to think about those moments now. They were so . . . soft. Sweet.

Neither of us are either of those things. Neither of us were *ever* either of those things.

How was it that together . . . we worked?

APHRA:
Sana. You'll *never* guess what happened today!

SANA STARROS:

Please don't tell me you went for it with the climbing wall again. It's like you *want* me to have a heart attack.

APHRA:

Never, sweet Sana. I like your heart the way it is—y'know, full of blood and valves and stuff. No, I got an offer! To go on my first archaeological expedition.

SANA STARROS:

That's incredible, love. Where to?

APHRA:

Weeeeelllll . . . I don't have the exact coordinates yet. It's all real top-secret stuff. But apparently, there's this old, abandoned fortress located on the most isolated edges of the Sarjenn system—

SANA STARROS:

You're not built for cold, you'll freeze to death—

APHRA:

Have you met me? I can survive *anything*. Or I'm sure I can buy a fetching new coat or something—

SANA STARROS:

And what do you mean "top-secret" and "apparently"? Is this a . . . sanctioned expedition? Has the leader filed the proper paperwork—

APHRA:

Um. Well. It might not be *exactly* sanctioned by . . . anyone—

SANA STARROS:

Wait. Who brought this to you? Where did the offer come from?

APHRA:

Here's the thing—

SANA STARROS:

Oh, *Aphra*. No. Don't tell me. It's some shady smuggler type who's offered to send you on a *death* expedition to dig up some incredibly valuable artifacts and will then pay you a truly disgusting amount of credits to do something terrible and probably illegal with them.

A beat of silence as Aphra looks away.

SANA STARROS:
Aphra?

APHRA:
You said not to tell you!

SANA STARROS:
Look. You're brilliant, you can do anything—why do you have to do things *this* way?

APHRA:
I just . . . I don't know.

SANA STARROS:
Tell you what. What if you and I do some research, file the paperwork, and go on the Sarjenn expedition ourselves? Aboveboard adventuring. Together.

APHRA:
I . . .

SANA STARROS:
Chelli. Please. I . . . I just want you to be safe. Sometimes I feel like I'm always at the bottom of that climbing wall, staring up at you. Wondering when you're going to fall.

APHRA:
But you were there to catch me.

SANA STARROS:
So let me catch you now.

APHRA (narration):
I stared into those beautiful brown eyes. It was like the day when our eyes first met, right after I'd tried to sneak into class. Only this time, she wasn't looking at me like I was out of my mind. No, she was so . . . open. She was *begging* me with that gaze.

She felt *safe* with me.

And I had never wanted anything more . . . than to say yes.

So I did.

APHRA:
Okay.

SANA STARROS:
Really?

APHRA:
Do I say things I don't mean? *Yes.*

SANA STARROS:
Oh, Chelli . . .

APHRA (narration):
Yeah, so. As you've probably figured out by now . . . I *always* say things I don't mean. I wish I could say, in this one particular instance, that I at least meant it in the moment.

But I was lying through my teeth.

I left the next day. No, it wasn't the first *or* the last time I lied to her . . . disappointed her . . . devastated her. There was plenty more of that to come. But it was one of the times I remember desperately wishing things could be different. That *I* could be different.

I skipped graduation—still got my doctorate, just didn't go to the ceremony. I didn't say goodbye, didn't even leave a note. I took that shady—but very wealthy—employer up on his offer. I went to Sarjenn Prime. It *was* cold—and this was another moment I almost died, because I almost froze myself into an early grave. But I did end up getting a fabulous coat.

At the time, I told myself it was all because the job was such an incredible challenge, such an *adventure*—and I wouldn't have to split the take.

But here's the truth: It was in that moment, when she . . . when *you* were looking at me so . . . openly, that I knew I had to leave. Because I wanted to say yes *so badly*.

Saying yes would have tied me to someone who made me weak.

And I could *not* be weak.

Like I said . . . this wasn't the first time I disappointed you, Sana Starros, and it most certainly wouldn't be the last. But that was the moment that rose up in my memory when I saw you again now . . . all that *hurt* flashing under the anger in your beautiful brown eyes . . . I knew.

I'd made you feel . . . well, the way I'd felt when Vader tried to kill me. Disposable. Worthless. A bug that could be stamped out without a second thought.

When I left . . . I should have at least told you what I was trying to do. That I'd wanted to keep *both* of us safe. And that I thought . . . no, I *knew* . . . that me leaving was the only way to do that.

Aphra's voice catches, and she struggles to hold back sobs.

APHRA (narration):
So. Let me try this again. The right way. Maybe the only time Chelli Lona Aphra has ever tried to do something the right way in all of her miserable life.

Recording: Encrypt this spot so I can't go back and delete it later.

Sana: I'm sorry. I *never* wanted to make you feel that way.

And I . . . I made this recording for you so maybe, just maybe . . . you would understand why I did what I did.

I never . . . felt nothing for you. That would be impossible.

I . . . I just . . .

I'm sorry.

Sana, please listen to me . . . if you hear nothing else on this recording, please hear that.

Please . . . *please* . . .

Aphra breaks off, unable to continue—crying herself to sleep.

SCENE 43. INT. APHRA'S CELL. SUNSPOT PRISON. MORNING.

APHRA (narration):
Ughhhh. So yeah. I basically cried myself to sleep in this tiny sun-soaked cell, this tiny piece of *hell*. How humiliating. Recording: Mark the previous sequence so I can decrypt it later. I know I made it extra hard to break, but . . . it's *me*. I'll figure it out. I break *everything*.

Now . . . back to pretending like I'm recording this for some generic, faceless person. I think you'd probably prefer that anyway, Sana.

When I awoke the next morning in my cell, I was pleased to find that I felt *refreshed*. Any traces of the previous night's angst-fest had been banished to the back of my mind. The cellar of my mind. The *dungeon*.

Sure, I was currently trapped in a horrifically hot prison and making sad faces over my ex, who most definitely wanted to kill me, but . . . I always find a way out. It's what I do.

If there's no door, I *make* one.

My mother, Amidala . . . their weakness came from their so-called goodness.

Luckily, I've never been *good*.

I called for chow time—only to realize there was a big ol' IG-RM thug droid outside my cell. And it was about to shoot at me! Apparently it did *not* speak the same mechanical language I did.

But then . . . something shot at the droid instead.

Hmph. I thought this prison was supposed to have amazing security!

Before I could ruminate on that too much, Princess *Annoying* showed up outside my cell . . .

PRINCESS LEIA:
Aphra—

APHRA:
Princess, if you're gonna kill me, at least have the guts to do it yourself instead of sending a droid to do your dirty work. That sounds like something *I* would do. Not *you,* your lawfulness.

PRINCESS LEIA:
If we wanted you dead, Aphra, we wouldn't be here.

SANA STARROS:
For the record, I'm perfectly fine with you being dead.

PRINCESS LEIA:
Stand back.

Leia fires at the cell door lock, freeing Aphra.

APHRA:
Yesssss, freedom!

SANA STARROS:
I still say this is a really bad idea. And I've been right the last five times I told you that.

PRINCESS LEIA:

We don't have any choice, Sana. Believe it or not, Doctor, we need your help. We're here to save you.

APHRA:

Save me? Save me from . . . ?

SANA STARROS:

This facility has been sieged by a murderous madman.

APHRA:

Excuse me, *what*?

SANA STARROS:

We don't know who he is or what he wants.

PRINCESS LEIA:

The way I see it, we either all work together or we all die. What do you say, Doctor? Feel like taking over a prison?

APHRA:

Heh. You're kidding, right? I was gonna do that anyway.

APHRA (narration):

Well, whaddya know. Sometimes doors come from the most unexpected places.

SCENE 44. INT. ADJACENT CELL BLOCK. SUNSPOT PRISON. LATER.

APHRA (narration):
While the princess skulked around trying to find a door for all of us, Sana and I booked it to the next cell block over—apparently there was some control panel doohickey over there that Sana was able to use to tap into the prison's comm line. Personally, I think she should have asked *me* to do it since I was always better at that kind of thing, but whatever! I was just happy to be free and in possession of my very own blaster rifle!

I'll admit I got kinda sorta distracted by yet another massive IG-RM droid stomping its way up to us—unfortunately, I was so fixated on its powerful gait, on its shiny armor, on all the things I could potentially *do* with such an amazing droid . . . that before I knew what was happening, it had its strong, grippy hands wrapped around Sana's neck.

I jumped into action immediately, popping open its back control panel to rewire it . . .

The IG-RM droid strangles Sana while Aphra frantically tries to re-wire it.

SANA STARROS:
Gaagh. Aphra! What are you doing? Get it off!

APHRA:
Hold still, Sana! I've almost got it.

APHRA (narration):
Hmm, so yes, this *does* look like I'm just letting a gigantic IG-RM droid strangle my ex-girlfriend, doesn't it? But actually . . . okay, fine, that's exactly what was happening. But I had my reasons.

SANA STARROS:
[struggling to breathe]

It's . . . choking . . . me . . .

APHRA:
I know. These things are *so* strong. Must have extra-strength pistons in the arms. Wow, I've never seen one in action before.

SANA STARROS:
Shoot . . . *it*! Shoot it in the . . .

APHRA:
Ah, don't be a baby. I've almost got—

A blaster fires, taking down the IG-RM droid.

APHRA:
Leia! What'd you do that for? I was rewiring it. I almost had us our very own IG-RM droid.

PRINCESS LEIA:
It was killing Sana.

APHRA:
I feel like you're focusing on the negative here, Princess. If you can call that a negative.

PRINCESS LEIA:

Play nice, Doctor Aphra, or I can't protect you from what's out there. Or from *her*.

APHRA:

Protect me? You guys can't even protect yourselves.

PRINCESS LEIA:

Sana, were you able to send the message?

SANA STARROS:

I'm gonna kill her. Let's see how *she* likes being strangled.

PRINCESS LEIA:

Sana! Focus, please.

SANA STARROS:

[grudging]

Not sure. Tapped into the prison's comm lines. Couldn't get a strong enough signal to reach the rebel fleet, but if there's somebody friendly in the area, we might get lucky.

Was busy trying to boost the signal when this droid jumped me.

Doc here let it walk right up on me.

APHRA:

I might still be able to fix it. I just need—

PRINCESS LEIA:

Get away from the droid, Doctor. That's not our mission.

APHRA:

I thought *staying alive* was our mission. Also, I don't remember agreeing to take orders from princesses.

PRINCESS LEIA:

You're still a *prisoner* here. Don't forget that.

If you'd rather take your chances in your cell than with us . . .

SANA STARROS:

I still say we throw her into the sun.

APHRA:

You do, sweetie, you might as well jump, too. Because without me, you two half-wits are as good as dead.

SANA STARROS:

I'll show you as good as dead!

PRINCESS LEIA:

Sana, stop it!

The prison is under siege by an unknown force. One who's determined to kill every prisoner he can. Our mission is to make sure *everyone* gets out of here alive.

And we're *failing*.

Everyone on this cell block is dead. So we move to the next one. Let's go.

SANA STARROS:

This is ridiculous. You're even crazier than she is. Why are we trying to save a bunch of prisoners? We need to be getting to the docking bay and getting out of here.

APHRA:

Or the armory. I'd be cool with going to the armory. As long as it's a big one.

PRINCESS LEIA:

We're not leaving. And I barely trust you with a rifle, Doctor, let alone anything bigger. Next cell block, ladies. *Move.*

SANA STARROS:

I am *so* gonna kill you before this is through, Aphra.

APHRA:

I've missed you, too, sweetie.

SCENE 45. INT. CORRIDOR. SUNSPOT PRISON. MOMENTS LATER.

APHRA (narration):
As it turned out, pretty much everyone in *every* cell block was dead. So we made a break for the prison's command center, the dead bodies of prisoners littering every cell block. And the mysterious intruder—the one Sana had called a "madman"—made his presence known, his voice echoing over the prison comm system . . .

ENEB RAY (on comm):
You're losing this battle, Princess. Which is why you're going to lose the war.

I will lead the way.

I am what you made me, Princess. I am a true soldier of the Alliance.

I am exactly what the galaxy needs.

APHRA:
Well, that sounds bad. Who is this guy, Princess?

PRINCESS LEIA:
I don't know.

APHRA:
Wow. The Rebellion is in even worse shape than I thought.

APHRA (narration):
We rounded the corner to the command center—which, naturally, was being guarded by a whole mess of pissed-off droids.

The droids open fire. Aphra, Sana, and Leia fire back.

SANA STARROS:
We'll never get those doors open! This was a terrible plan!

APHRA:
There was a plan?

PRINCESS LEIA:
Just keep shooting!

APHRA:
My kind of plan!

SANA STARROS:
Just one last droid, but he's got us pinned down!

APHRA:
Last droid? That's not the last droid!

APHRA (narration):
It sure wasn't! Because right then, my glorious IG-RM droid, the one I'd been trying to rewire while Sana was busy getting strangled, clomped down the hall and marched straight up to that last droid guarding the control room doors . . .

SANA STARROS:
Uh-oh.

APHRA:
See? I told you I was rewiring it.

APHRA (narration):
The droid guarding the door tried to have a special bonding moment with my IG-RM—

GUARD DROID:
WWWWRZZZTTT!

APHRA (narration):
But my IG-RM was way more special. And he didn't want to bond. He *blasted* that inferior guard droid . . . and me, Sana, and the princess stormed the command center!

PRINCESS LEIA:
Nobody move!

SANA STARROS:
Move once, you won't be moving again.

APHRA:
Hi. I'm not a rebel, but I'll still shoot you.

APHRA (narration):
It was not quite the badass scene we'd imagined. Skywalker's annoying droids—the Triple-Zero and Beetee doppelgängers—were hanging out amongst more dead bodies.

C-3PO:
Ahh, help! I'm fighting for my life!

R2-D2:
BUDDA BUDDA THWRRK!

PRINCESS LEIA:
Artoo, plug in and take control of the prison!

APHRA:
Well, don't all thank me at once.

SANA STARROS:
Oh, I'll thank you all right. Right after I shoot that IG-RM thing in the face. Move aside, Doc.

APHRA:

You can't kill him, Sana! Not my beautiful IG-RM droid! He saved us all!

SANA STARROS:

Move aside, I said.

APHRA:

Come off it, Sana. This isn't about the droid. What happened between us was a long time ago. You should learn to get over your crushes!

SANA STARROS:

And you should grow some guts and learn to stab people in the *front* for a change!

Last warning. *Stand aside,* Aphra.

PRINCESS LEIA:

Everybody stop yelling but me! I'm trying to figure out who's behind this—

HAN SOLO (on comm):

Sounds like we got here just in time.

PRINCESS LEIA:

What? Han? Is that you? Are you . . . where are you?

HAN SOLO (on comm):

Headed for the Sunspot Prison docking bay. Luke and I got your message. So relax, will ya, Your Highness? We're here to save the day.

APHRA (narration):

Oh, great. Han Solo—here to swoop in, do absolutely nothing, and take all the credit!

SCENE 46. INT. DOCKING BAY. SUNSPOT PRISON. MOMENTS LATER.

APHRA (narration):
Sure enough, as soon as we got to the docking bay where big, bad Han Solo was supposedly waiting to save us all from danger, we discovered that the intruder, the man behind this murderous prison break, had captured both Han and the Skywalker kid, knocking them out cold.

This so-called madman who'd taken over the prison so handily was outfitted in a full-body spacesuit and helmet that covered his entire face. And his voice was muffled and flat, giving nothing away.

I suppose he thought the blaster pointed at us said plenty.

ENEB RAY:
I'm sorry, Princess.

APHRA:
This is . . . wow . . . how you people aren't all *dead* already is seriously the greatest mystery in the galaxy.

PRINCESS LEIA:
Let Han and Luke go. *Now.*

ENEB RAY:
I'm sorry, Princess. But that isn't how this ends.

This is your last chance to accept what I've been trying to show you, Princess Leia. I want you to win this war, I really do. I want to see the Empire fall. I want to give you the tools you need for victory.

Whether your friends here become casualties in that war is entirely up to you.

PRINCESS LEIA:
Don't do it.

Don't hurt them. Look, I'll put my blaster down, and then we can talk about—

ENEB RAY:
I don't want you to put it down. I want you to *use* it.

I want you to show me you have what it takes to lead the Rebellion. You have an Imperial prisoner in your midst. *Shoot her!* And I'll let your friends go free.

APHRA:
Wait. *What?*

PRINCESS LEIA:
That's not what's going to happen—

SANA STARROS:
Yes, it is.

APHRA:
Sana! Are you really pointing a blaster at my head? After everything we've been through together . . .

SANA STARROS:
As I said before, Aphra: Our old times were never that great.

APHRA:

I meant in the last five minutes! That bit we developed? About the IG-RM droid trying to kill you, and then you trying to kill the droid . . . it's so *us*! Can't you feel the *connection*—

SANA STARROS:

No. Sorry, Aphra, nothing personal.

APHRA:

Murder is always personal, Sana! Especially when it's *mine*!

PRINCESS LEIA:

Sana! This is not happening! This is not who we are!

SANA STARROS:

Speak for yourself, Princess.

APHRA:

No, really. This *is* who she is.

ENEB RAY:

If this isn't who you are, Princess Leia, then we're doomed. The entire Rebellion.

PRINCESS LEIA:

Sana, put down that blaster! And you, *whoever* you are, stop trying to—

ENEB RAY:

I am who *you* made me, Princess. You *sent* me to them.

APHRA (narration):

The mysterious intruder removed his helmet. His face wasn't one I recognized. Humanoid. Scarred. Eyes so haunted, I had to look away.

ENEB RAY:

You can't be surprised that I came back *changed*.

PRINCESS LEIA:

No. It can't . . . Eneb? Eneb Ray . . . ?

APHRA:
Are we supposed to know who that is?

SANA STARROS:
I can't hear you, you're already dead.

PRINCESS LEIA:
Eneb, what . . .

ENEB RAY:
So you *do* remember me?

PRINCESS LEIA:
You were one of us. The best spy we ever put in the field. After
Coruscant, we looked all over for you. We thought you must have
died with the others.

ENEB RAY:
Oh, his touch will definitely kill me. It's just going to take its time.

PRINCESS LEIA:
Whose touch? Eneb, what's happened to you? You need to come
home and let us help—

ENEB RAY:
I'm not the one who needs help, Princess. You've got five seconds
to save your friends. And this war.

Kill the Imperial. Or your friends die.

APHRA:
Wait a second! I'm not *technically* an Imperial . . .

ENEB RAY:
One!

PRINCESS LEIA:
Wait . . . Eneb, please . . .

ENEB RAY:
Two!

SANA STARROS:
Princess, if you won't take care of this, I will—

PRINCESS LEIA:
No, Sana, don't you—

ENEB RAY:
Three!

SANA STARROS:
Sorry, Aphra. Sorta.

APHRA:
You'd kill *me* to save *Solo*? Really?

ENEB RAY:
Four!

PRINCESS LEIA:
I'm sorry I failed you, Eneb. But I'm not about to fail my friends.

ENEB RAY:
You just did. *Five.*

PRINCESS LEIA:
Artoo! *Now!*

R2-D2 (on comm):
WHRRR-BOOP!

C-3PO (on comm):
Oh, thank the Maker. I finally feel like I've recovered my bearings after that vicious bout of hand-to-hand combat. What's happening? Is that Princess Leia I'm hearing?

R2-D2 (on comm):
WHRR-WOO WEE BOOP!

C-3PO (on comm):
What do you mean I should hold on to something?

R2-D2 knocks out the prison's gravity with an ion pulse.

ENEB RAY:

Wha . . . Why are we *floating*?

PRINCESS LEIA:

Ion pulse. No gravity. Your trigger's down, Eneb. And so are you.

Leia punches Eneb in the face.

APHRA:

Damn, the princess has a mean left hook. Better grab on to something . . .

SANA STARROS:

Whoa . . . what the . . .

APHRA:

Gravity's gone. The whole prison just shut down. We'll fall into the star.

SANA STARROS:

Don't worry. You'll be dead long before then.

Sana wraps her hands around Aphra's throat.

APHRA:

[struggling to breathe]

When I said "grab on to something," I didn't mean *my neck,* Sana! I'm starting to feel like . . . this isn't the fight . . . we should be fighting.

SANA STARROS:

Funny how you didn't say that before my hands were on your throat. And I didn't wanna fight. I just want to kill you.

APHRA:

Okay. *Okay.* I'm sorry, Sana. I really am. I'm sorry about the way I left things. If you were a blaster, I would've known how to deal with you. Blasters I know. But people—

SANA STARROS:

Save it, Aphra. Save your last, miserable breaths. Dealing with people would require you to *care.*

APHRA:

I . . . I did care! I really did! Sana, from the moment I first saw you . . . I cared.

SANA STARROS:

Shut *up*, Aphra!

APHRA:

But I just . . . I never knew what I was doing, and you know I'm not great at thinking ahead, and . . . and I knew I was probably about to be expelled at any moment anyway!

I'm still shocked Sava Toob-Nix didn't boot me after I back-talked him in class that day . . .

SANA STARROS:

He didn't boot you because *I* told him not to!

APHRA:

Wh-what?

SANA STARROS:

I went to his office later that day—and I told him if he expelled you, I'd report the fact that he'd tried to teach us something completely erroneous. That he'd pretended to be ignorant to existing research, just because it furthered his own academic agenda. I told him he'd be *done*.

APHRA:

Y-you blackmailed someone? For *me*?

SANA STARROS:

Yes, and I've never regretted anything more.

APHRA:

Sana . . . please. I'm sorry about everything. We need to . . . *guuuk*, you're still choking me. Did you hear what I—

SANA STARROS:

You're sorry, huh? I'll show you sorry, Doc.

APHRA:
Whaaaaaaaa!

APHRA (narration):
She flung me away from her with such force . . . For a second, I thought she was trying to *save* me. That she couldn't bring herself to actually kill me.

And I felt . . . something soft. And sweet. After all these years.

Studious Sana had blackmailed someone. For *me*.

Is this . . . what love feels like?

But as it turned out, Sana was throwing me directly into the path of Eneb Ray, knocking him away from the princess.

I punched him in the gut. Just 'cause.

But the princess got the final blow in, knocking him out.

PRINCESS LEIA:
We *will* win, Eneb. Because there are more of us than you can count. And we're all sick to damn death of being told what to do.

SCENE 47. INT. SUNSPOT PRISON. LATER.

APHRA (narration):
Yeah, so we saved the prison! Well, sort of. I mean, it still shut down right after that. But at least some of us escaped with our lives.

PRISON WARDEN:
Prison systems have been restored. And the evacuation has begun. Thanks to you, Princess, there are still some of us left to evacuate.

PRINCESS LEIA:
But not enough. Too many people died here today, Warden. Guards and prisoners both.

PRISON WARDEN:
Yes, we're doing our best to account for all of the remaining inmates. But, ah . . . I'm afraid there is *one* that seems to have been misplaced.

APHRA (narration):
Hmmm, who could he be talking about? No idea.

Oh, right. It was me! While the princess was brooding away about some unhinged rebel spy she hadn't managed to save, I was booking it for my door—an untended escape pod.

But because she couldn't leave well enough alone, the princess was hot on my heels. And right before I was set to leap into the escape pod's warm embrace, she showed up with a blaster.

PRINCESS LEIA:
Get away from the escape pod, Doctor Aphra.

APHRA:
Oh, c'mon. I saved your life like five times today! Way more if you count all the times I didn't kill you when I really wanted to.

PRINCESS LEIA:
That doesn't change the fact that you're a *prisoner* here. I can't just let you walk away.

APHRA:
Um, yes, you definitely could.

What if I promise to be good? Or . . . you know . . . at least better than usual?

PRINCESS LEIA:
This is no game, Doctor. I hope you realize just how dangerous Darth Vader really is. No matter how useful you are to him now, sooner or later he will get around to killing you.

And when that day comes, if you should happen to somehow survive . . . I suggest you look me up.

APHRA:
Wait, but . . . what are you saying?

PRINCESS LEIA:
I said *I* couldn't let you walk away. I didn't say anything about *her.*

APHRA:
Whu . . .

APHRA (narration):
And there she was again . . . there *you* were. Damn, Sana, you looked at me like you could see directly into my soul. And you were *mad* about what you saw.

You kicked me in the midsection. *Hard.* And I went flying into the escape pod.

COMPUTER VOICE:
Escape pod activated.

SANA STARROS:
And don't ever come back.

SCENE 48. INT. BAR. THE COSMATANIC STEPPES. THE OUTER RIM. DAY.

Atmosphere: Light conversation and the occasional clink of glasses. A sadder, more abandoned, less rowdy type of bar—but more real. There's something comforting about it, especially for someone who wants to disappear. It should feel like we're on the very edge of the galaxy.

BARTENDER:
Back already, miss? Isn't it a little early?

APHRA:
The best thing about multi-sun systems, friend? My no-drinks-before-noon rule is *wayyy* easier to follow. Hit me.

BARTENDER:
You've got one hell of a tab to settle . . .

APHRA (narration):
Yeah, so. I found the most abandoned, hole-in-the-galaxy bar I could out in the Cosmatanic Steppes. I knew Vader would be look-

ing for me. And this time, I had nothing to bring him, no triumphs, nothing to show for my efforts.

And I certainly knew at this point that he didn't harbor any special, fuzzy feelings for me or my talents.

I . . . had to admit to myself, during one of my drunken binges, that I don't think he ever actually *saw* me. I, like so many others, was a mere pawn in his game, a speck of dust to be brushed aside once she'd outlived her usefulness.

And at this point? I'd definitely outlived . . . many things.

"More lives than a tooka-cat," eh? But even tooka-cats die eventually.

I couldn't think of anything to do but *run*.

Yeah, your old pal Aphra was feeling pretty down when she got to the Cosmatanic Steppes. There wasn't really anything to do except drown my sorrows in booze.

The bartender was a kind sort—in other words, he had no business being a bartender. But he let me drink till the wee hours, and he accepted the droids I scavenged as credit.

APHRA:
Found this little fella in the remains outside. Got him back on his feet. Droid for a few drinks sounds like a good deal to me . . .

BARTENDER:
Sure, miss, sure . . . But you know . . . when someone drinks like you have, I can tell they're hiding. Especially when you won't even give me your name.

What are you running from? It can't be that bad.

APHRA (narration):
Sure, barkeep, not that bad. Not that bad at all. I'm only wanted by the Dark Lord of the Sith, pursued across the galaxy by all the bounty hunters he's probably hired, and currently caught in the unending spiral of an existential crisis after seeing my ex . . .

Shooting outside interrupts the peacefulness of the bar.

APHRA:
Oh, what now? That can't be about me, right?

APHRA (narration):
I peeked out the window . . . and saw my old friends, Triple-Zero and Beetee, flanked by a whole battalion of commando droids.

So it *was* about me.

APHRA:
Oh no. Triple-Zero, what are you doing?

TRIPLE-ZERO:
Eliminating witnesses. Master Vader was very specific about making sure you hadn't spread word to anyone else. Who knows what you could have said in one of your drunken binges, Mistress Aphra?

APHRA:
The rebels captured me. I escaped. I didn't tell anyone anything!

TRIPLE-ZERO:
Well done! I'm sure you'll find not telling anyone anything a far less demanding task when you're safely disposed of, mistress.

APHRA:
Wait! I'm your master! You take my orders. Stand down! *Now!*

TRIPLE-ZERO:
First rule of protocol droids: protocol. We have a *priority* order from our *other* master. We must deal with our priority order before progressing to anything else.

BEETEE:
BLEEP!

TRIPLE-ZERO:
I'm afraid we're going to have to hunt you down like the human meatbag you are, Mistress Aphra. I'm sorry, but I am such a terrible stickler.

APHRA:

Okay!

[sotto]

Think, Aphra, think . . .

[normal voice]

What was the specific order?

TRIPLE-ZERO:

Why, to bring you to the *Executor* to await Master Vader, and failing that, to silence you.

APHRA:

Hmm. Okay. So . . . I surrender.

TRIPLE-ZERO:

Hmmph. Stand down, everyone.

Mistress Aphra, I have to say, you do take the fun out of everything.

BEETEE:

BLEEP!

TRIPLE-ZERO:

Beetee is very upset.

APHRA:

[sotto]

Time to find another door.

SCENE 49. INT. THE *EXECUTOR*. LATER.

APHRA (narration):
They took me to Vader's new ship: the *Executor*. A Super Star Destroyer. Oh, and did I mention that my old pal Black Krrsantan
was part of this whole "let's bring Aphra in so Vader can murder
her" expedition? The *nerve*. I thought we'd bonded.

It was, in fact, *his* ship that transported me to my doom. I saw all
those ingots from the Son-tuul Pride robbery—the ingots I'd so
nicely given him—scattered everywhere, their beautiful prism
glow mocking me.

BLACK KRRSANTAN:
HHHHHRRHHHHH!

APHRA:
Yeah, great to see you, too, Santy. Any chance I can bribe you into
helping me?

BLACK KRRSANTAN:
HRRRNNFF!

APHRA:

Yeah, I didn't think so.

TRIPLE-ZERO:

If I can be so bold, Mistress Aphra, I suspect you'll soon regret your decision to surrender. There are far worse fates than death by blaster, and I'm sure that Master Vader has one in mind.

BEETEE:

BLEEP!

TRIPLE-ZERO:

Yes, Beetee, and if he hasn't, we certainly have suggestions.

Notice I didn't say you'd *live* to regret this?

APHRA:

I did.

TRIPLE-ZERO:

Just making sure. I do tend to overuse subtext. It's *terrible* to miss the subtext.

BLACK KRRSANTAN:

GRRRRWWWWWWWW!

APHRA (narration):

My traitorous former colleagues marched me over to some storm-troopers.

TRIPLE-ZERO:

This is Doctor Aphra. Lord Vader ordered us to bring her here. Keep her safely locked away for him, hmm?

Goodness, Mistress Aphra. It's been a pleasure.

APHRA:

Triple-Zero! I'm to be safely delivered to the *Executor,* right? That was the priority order?

TRIPLE-ZERO:

That you are, Mistress Aphra! Nice and safely *doomed*!

APHRA:

Then your priority order to Vader is complete! *New* priority order . . .

Get me out of here!

BEETEE:
BLEEP!

TRIPLE-ZERO:
Quite. How *annoying*.

Very well, Mistress Aphra, Beetee and I are now here to save you!
The cavalry has arrived!

APHRA:
After . . . delivering me to my death.

TRIPLE-ZERO:
One cannot be too choosy about *which* cavalry arrives when you're
in this position, Mistress Aphra! I suggest you take it.

And . . . may I just say, for an organic . . . your plan with the priority order was rather clever.

APHRA:
It was barely a plan, but thanks all the same. So how are you guys
gonna liberate me?

BEETEE:
BLEEP! BLEEP BLEEP!

TRIPLE-ZERO:
Well, I don't know about that, Beetee, releasing a human-targeted
neurotoxin would take out everyone around us—but it would also
take out Mistress Aphra!

BEETEE:
BLEEEEEP!

TRIPLE-ZERO:
What do you mean you've already begun?

APHRA:
Oh . . . *Void* . . .

As Beetee releases his toxic gas, Aphra passes out.

SCENE 50. INT. HOLDING CELL. THE *EXECUTOR*. LATER.

APHRA (narration):
Why did I keep waking up in cells? I couldn't remember losing consciousness. One minute, I was yelling. The next, my eyes were fluttering open and my body was draped across a very cold floor.

BEETEE:
BLEEP! BLEEP!

TRIPLE-ZERO:
Yes, please do wake up, Mistress Aphra. Beetee is getting tetchy.

APHRA:
Whhhh . . .

TRIPLE-ZERO:
We appear to have rescued you. Without murdering anyone, too. Something of a disappointment, truth be told.

APHRA:
Wha . . . what happened, Triple-Zero? I . . . passed out. Was it some kind of . . . gas?

TRIPLE-ZERO:

Correct. A human-targeted neurotoxin. Highly permeable across safety filters. I'm genuinely impressed. Everyone who hasn't received an antidote from their mostly faithful droid assistant is unconscious.

BEETEE:

BLEEP! BLEEP! BLEEP!

TRIPLE-ZERO:

Oh, calm down, Beetee! I was getting to that! Yes, obviously, it's ineffective against nonhumans or droids. Ah, the disadvantage of a monoculture. Once more, I have to question the wisdom of replacing the droid armies with fleshy ones.

All this embarrassing slumping didn't happen back in the days of the former Republic. Anyway—with everyone lying drooling on the floor, we should be able to escape with relative ease. Black Krrsantan is docked, awaiting us . . .

A rumble passes through the ship.

APHRA:

I know my head's not straight, but . . . did the ship just *move*?

TRIPLE-ZERO:

Correct. If I'm not mistaken, someone is stealing the *Executor*, and is presumably responsible for all the chaos. I have to admit . . . I *do* feel a certain spark of professional jealousy.

APHRA:

I . . . really, why bother? I can run, but Vader's not going to let me get away.

TRIPLE-ZERO:

This is true, Mistress Aphra. Doesn't matter particularly to us, of course. As long as *someone* dies, we're just dandy.

IMPERIAL OFFICER (on comm):

Squad Pheno-Six. Converge on the Emperor's quarters and bring him to the bridge.

APHRA (narration):

And there it was. My door.

APHRA:

Trip, I need you to do something for me.

TRIPLE-ZERO:

We're not leaving, Mistress Aphra?

APHRA:

Not yet. I've had another one of my patented never-go-wrong ideas.

APHRA (narration):

Ooooof. I probably should have called it . . . my worst idea yet.

I didn't know exactly what was behind this particular door.

But I *did* know it was my only possible way out.

SCENE 51. INT. EMPEROR'S CHAMBERS. THE *EXECUTOR*. LATER.

Emperor Palpatine sits on his throne, flanked by guards.

EMPEROR PALPATINE:
You have completed your task, Lord Vader?

DARTH VADER (on comm):
Yes, Master. The ship is secured.

EMPEROR PALPATINE:
Good. Please return. There is much to discuss.

DARTH VADER (on comm):
Yes, Master.

APHRA (narration):
Remember how impressed I was with Darth Vader's dramatic entrance into my life? Once I was sure I'd heard his comm disconnect . . . I made mine.

APHRA:
There *is* much to discuss, your Emperor Highness Master Sir!

EMPEROR PALPATINE:

Who *dares* intrude into my private chambers?

APHRA:

I'm Doctor Aphra. Sorry, didn't mean to break in. Did you know the triple lock on your door is *really* easy to disengage? Probably want to get that looked at.

EMPEROR PALPATINE:

Such insolence! I don't know what you think you're going to accomplish—

APHRA:

We've got a mutual friend. I've got things you *need* to know.

EMPEROR PALPATINE:

I am quite certain we have *nothing* in common.

APHRA:

You'd be surprised, your majesticness. So let me tell you a little story about my best friend and yours . . . Darth Vader.

[beat]

That's your cue to act all shocked. Hold on, I probably didn't do it right, let me say that again, with extra drama: *Darth*—

EMPEROR PALPATINE:

I'm listening. I suggest you take advantage of this opportunity.

APHRA:

Ahhh, *opportunity.* One of my favorite words.

See, Darth Vader *also* presented me with an opportunity. To become his super-secret attaché. We had *so much fun.* Built a secret droid army, robbed the Empire, and killed a bunch of people. All in the name of building Vader's power once more!

And we did it all . . . behind your back.

EMPEROR PALPATINE:

This is a very . . . interesting tale. But obviously a lie. Vader would never betray me so . . . so *blatantly.*

APHRA:

Oh, but he would, your all-powerfulness. I mean. Think about it. He's *Darth Vader*. He never does anything halfway. And you probably taught him how to execute all this stealthy trickery so . . . masterfully.

The apprentice has become—

EMPEROR PALPATINE:

You will regret finishing that sentence.

APHRA:

Riiiiiight. Sorry, sometimes I just get really excited when I'm telling a good story.

Anywaaaaaay, given my up close and personal access to Vader's recent secret exploits . . . I thought maybe I could share some of the finer details with you. I know *a lot*.

EMPEROR PALPATINE:

Mmm. Perhaps you could. Continue.

APHRA:

Awww, Mr. Emperor, sir. I feel like we're about to become very good friends.

SCENE 52. INT. EMPEROR'S CHAMBERS. THE *EXECUTOR*. LATER.

APHRA (narration):
Much later, Vader entered ol' Palpy's chamber. By then, Palpy and I were the best of friends . . .

DARTH VADER:
My task is complete, the *Executor* is secured. Is there anything else you require, my Master?

EMPEROR PALPATINE:
I was hoping for a full report . . . but your *aide* has been most helpful in filling in the gaps.

DARTH VADER:
Aide . . . ?

APHRA:
Why did you never introduce me to your boss, boss? The Emperor's one hell of a guy.

EMPEROR PALPATINE:

Creating your own Empire within the Empire? Securing finances by open robbery from Imperial treasures? Covering up the crime by slaughtering those who would expose you?

APHRA:

Oh boy, are *you* in trouble.

EMPEROR PALPATINE:

Most *impressive*, Vader.

You let your anger and pride guide you to the darkest places. That is our way. All you did in the shadows is most pleasing to me. You are everything I could have hoped for.

I'm sure you'll want . . . some words with Doctor Aphra. Meet me on the bridge afterward. There is more to speak of.

APHRA:

Wait . . . *what*? *No!* This is not how this is supposed to go! Emperor . . . your majesty . . . please . . . I can tell you more . . ,

EMPEROR PALPATINE:

Come to me after you have taken care of your lapdog, Vader.

DARTH VADER:

Walk with me, Aphra.

APHRA:

I . . . I . . . you have to understand, boss. I didn't *want* to betray you, but you didn't exactly leave me many options. I figured, prove myself to the Emperor, get on *your* boss's good side, and he'd protect me from you. He'd give you the slap on the wrist for your bad-boy antics, and then we could get back to normal.

But he loves it. I've *proved* you to him.

And I didn't betray your *real* secret—whatever's going on with that rebel kid!

So things couldn't have ended better for you, boss! You understand, yeah?

APHRA (narration):
I couldn't tell if he was hearing me at all. He just kept walking down a long, long hall as I babbled and tried to keep up with him.

That *silence*. Always so much worse than any words he could say.

And then, suddenly . . . we were there. At my worst nightmare.

The air lock.

And he was looking at me in *that way* again. Like I was *nothing*. A lapdog. A worthless "mechanic." A bug to be squashed.

DARTH VADER:
Enter.

Vader opens the air lock.

APHRA:
The . . . air lock.

No! *No!*

You promised me the saber! Nice and quick!

Vader shoves Aphra into the air lock.

APHRA:
You promised!

DARTH VADER:
I promised you nothing.

Vader seals Aphra in the air lock.

APHRA:
I did everything you wanted! And more! *You can't!*

Not like this. Please, not like this.

Please, please . . .

Vader launches Aphra into space.

APHRA (narration):
It was cold. So *cold*. Somehow even colder than I'd imagined it.

Such an odd sensation, going from being stuffed into a cramped, claustrophobic space, feeling my blood roar through my veins, hearing my heartbeat thrumming louder . . . and louder . . .

And then suddenly . . . that *cold*.

I couldn't feel anything. I could feel everything.

The vastness of space looks . . . different when there's nothing between you and the stars.

I've never felt so . . . alone.

And I had that moment of terror, the one I'd been running from all my life.

As I drifted through the endless black, I knew: My face looked exactly like my mother's before she died.

SCENE 53. INT. BLACK KRRSANTAN'S SHIP. MOMENTS LATER.

APHRA (narration):
This time I'm dead. Definitely, definitely dead.

And I know you're probably asking: So how are you recording this, then, oh great and powerful and ingenious Doctor Aphra?

Do you know me *at all*?

The answer, of course . . . is that I'm not *quite* dead.

BEETEE:
BLEEP!

TRIPLE-ZERO:
No, I'm not exactly sure how long a human can stay alive while exposed to a hard vacuum. But now is not the time to indulge in your experimental mindset, Beetee. There she is! Retract her aboard! Swiftly!

BLACK KRRSANTAN:
HHHHHRRRRRRWWWW!

TRIPLE-ZERO:

Yes, quite. Your ship *does* have many fine attributes, Mr. Krrsantan, perfect for a rescue mission. Are you alive, Mistress Aphra?

APHRA:

Maybe. You can have your ingots back, Krrsantan. They shielded me against the deadly atmosphere of space quite nicely, just the way I . . . well, I didn't totally know they would. I'm done.

TRIPLE-ZERO:

I have to admit, I'm impressed, Mistress Aphra. Having Master Vader eject you into space, and reusing the equipment from the Son-tuul Pride robbery to retrieve you? Elegantly done.

APHRA:

What can I say, guys? Crushing fear of imminent death is a great motivator. And I knew you still had a soft spot for me, Santy.

Only way Vader'd let me go was if he thought I was dead. Only way he'd think I was dead is if he'd killed me.

TRIPLE-ZERO:

Hmm. Of course, he might have always used the saber.

APHRA:

He's Darth Vader. He was *never* going to be kind.

APHRA (narration):

Yeah, so. Maybe I kind of, sort of hatched a pretty incredible master plan. See, while I was angsting my way through the entire liquor stock of the Cosmatanic Steppes bar . . . it *really* hit me that Vader was never going to let me go. He'd swat me like a fly as soon as he laid eyes on me.

And not just because I'd assisted him in a little light treason and gotten myself captured by the rebels.

I think he also knew, after I pressed him on Vrogas Vas . . . that I was close to figuring out his deepest secret. The one about the kid—Skywalker.

Something stuck with me about Luke's natterings to his little R2 unit. When they were exploring the Jedi temple ruins, he'd said he *sensed* someone important nearby. And yeah, sure . . . he could have meant some Force magic kind of thing.

But his voice kept echoing through my head as I pounded yet another Corellian whiskey shot . . .

LUKE SKYWALKER:
My father—I sense my father.

APHRA (narration):
It all made sense. Vader's obsession. The way he'd said he also "sensed" Luke on Vrogas Vas. Everything.

That was it. That was the secret.

That was the only thing he cared about—the only thing he'd *ever* care about.

I was right all along—the kid was the crack in Vader's armor. The key to unlocking his weakness.

I figured if I betrayed Vader to the Emperor . . . well, I didn't totally know the outcome, but I was pretty sure one of two things would happen. Either the Emperor would take me on as his new attaché and send Vader out the air lock—or he'd finally truly see Vader for the boss he is. And then Vader would send *me* out the air lock.

Which I was totally ready for.

I stuffed my jacket full of Black Krrsantan's ingots from the Sontuul Pride robbery—the better to protect my fragile organic body as it plummeted through space—and then asked Santy to use the same satellite/retrieval technique we'd used during the robbery to bring me on board his ship.

So . . . why didn't I tell the Emperor about Skywalker?

Welllll . . . like I said, it's Vader's deepest, darkest secret. And I need to have *something* up my sleeve in case he ever finds me again.

Call it an insurance policy. Call it *survival.*

Although . . . I don't think I want to be Vader's attaché again. I don't think I want to be *anyone's* attaché. I'd like to be my own boss for a while, thanks—and as my only employee, I think I'm gonna be pretty awesome at it.

I kept thinking Vader truly *saw* me . . . just like I've wanted so many people in my life to see me. And I have to admit . . . it felt *good.* I kept thinking it would help me . . . access his power, somehow. Use it for myself. And then I'd never be cold or hungry or lonely ever again.

I'd never be *weak.*

But I don't want to be powerful by association anymore. I just want to be powerful, period. And I think Chelli Lona Aphra is more than up to the task.

I finally see *myself.* And that's all I need!

Cue dramatic music, annnnd . . . end recording!

A beat as the recording seems to end.

APHRA (narration):
Resume recording.

Wait, wait . . . no. That's not the end.

I just . . . I can't . . .

Oh, Sana.

Remember my angsty moment, sitting all alone in my cell in Sunspot Prison, wondering how I was going to find a way out?

I guess . . . in addition to this paving the way for my eventual master plan . . . well, there was something else I realized. This . . . desperation, this *need* to find a door . . . meant that I actually really, wholeheartedly wanted to *live.* That as glib as I was about dying by the saber, I actually didn't want to die, period.

And I also realized that one of the reasons I didn't want to die in that moment . . . was the way I left things with *you*.

I regret us, Sana. Not that we *were* us. That I couldn't let us *continue* to be us. That I couldn't let myself be weak with you. That I left instead of telling you how much I cared.

Sana, I'm so sorry.

I . . . I don't think I ever knew that *you* actually saw me. You knew I could be . . . everything. You *blackmailed* someone for me, for Void's sake.

My sweet, studious Sana . . . I made this for you.

But you won't hear it until I'm *actually* dead.

And if I have anything to say about it . . . that won't be for a very long time.

[beat]

Okay, *now* end recording. For real this time.

TRIPLE-ZERO:
Well, mistress, now that we've rescued you—what's next? We're very excited for the next death-defying adventure! Hopefully there will be more murder this time, though . . .

BEETEE:
BLEEP BLEEP!

BLACK KRRSANTAN:
RAAAAAWRGGGH!

APHRA:
Thanks for the enthusiasm, boys. Now get me to the bacta tank. And get us out of here.

And . . . that was fun.

Let's never do it again.

ACKNOWLEDGMENTS

It was an honor to write Doctor Chelli Lona Aphra, chaos princess-adventurer and one of the best *Star Wars* characters ever. Thank you to my amazing editor, Elizabeth Schaefer, for believing I was the right person for the job and guiding me through every step with care. And to Nick Martorelli, audio producer extraordinaire, for making Aphra's world come together so vividly.

Thank you to Emily Woo Zeller, who truly brought Aphra to life, and made us all laugh and cry and feel every possible emotion while doing so. And to the rest of the incredible cast—Jonathan Davis, Sean Patrick Hopkins, Sean Kenin, Nicole Lewis, Carol Monda, Euan Morton, Catherine Taber, and Marc Thompson—for giving such beautiful performances as characters both classic and new.

Thank you to Kieron Gillen and Salvador Larroca for creating an icon and giving me a wonderful tale to work with, and to the many great creators who have worked on Aphra over the years—especially Simon Spurrier, Alyssa Wong, Heather Antos, Jordan D. White, Leinil Francis Yu, Mike Deodato, and Jason Aaron. And to Jennifer Heddle, Matt Martin, Emily Shkoukani, and everyone at Lucasfilm and Del Rey for helping me make this book the best it could be. Thank you to Nicole Morano for handling several kerzillion publicity requests; to my agent, Diana Fox, for helping make my *Star Wars* dreams come true; and to all of Aphra's many enthusiastic fans, who made this experience delightful.

Thank you to all the friends and family who have fed and enhanced my love of this franchise over the years. Special shout-outs to Jenn Fujikawa, Amy Ratcliffe, Christine Dinh, Andrea Letamendi, Christy Black, Mel Caylo, Rebekah Weatherspoon, and Javier Grillo-Marxuach, who all contributed to this particular book in ways great and small.

And thank you to Jeff Chen, who makes it all possible—and who loves droids just as much as Aphra does.

ABOUT THE AUTHOR

SARAH KUHN is the author of the popular Heroine Complex novels—a series starring Asian American superheroines. The first book is a Locus bestseller, an RT Reviewers' Choice Award nominee, and one of the Barnes & Noble Sci-Fi & Fantasy Blog's Best Books of 2016. Her YA debut, the Japan set romantic comedy *I Love You So Mochi*, is a Junior Library Guild selection and a nominee for YALSA's Best Fiction for Young Adults. She has also penned a variety of short fiction and comics, including the critically acclaimed graphic novel *Shadow of the Batgirl* for DC Comics. Additionally, she was a finalist for both the CAPE (Coalition of Asian Pacifics in Entertainment) New Writers Award and the Astounding Award for Best New Writer. A third-generation Japanese American, she lives in Los Angeles with her husband and an overflowing closet of vintage treasures.

Facebook.com/sarahkuhnbooks
Twitter: @sarahkuhn

Read on for an excerpt from

DOOKU

JEDI LOST

BY CAVAN SCOTT

NARRATOR:

A long time ago in a galaxy far, far away. . . .

CUE THEME

SCENE 1. INT. CASTLE SERENNO. KEEP. NIGHT.

Atmosphere: Wind whistles past a balcony, high in Dooku's castle.

VENTRESS: (NARRATION)
I hate it here.

I hate the castle. I hate the cliff. I hate the spikebats whirling above the forest far below. I hate the moons grinning down at me.

I hate the fact that night after night I stand on this ledge, feeling the breeze against my skin, wondering what it would be like to jump, to drop down into the trees.

Would the Force guide me?

Would it help me find that perfect branch that would take my weight so I could spring to safety, leaves crunching beneath my feet as I ran, rodents scurrying for their nests.

KY NAREC: (GHOST)
How did you get here, little one?

VENTRESS: (NARRATION)
Most of all, I hate that voice. The stupid, impossible voice. A voice of the past. A voice that doesn't belong.

KY NAREC: (GHOST)
I said . . .

VENTRESS:
I know what you said, Ky.

KY NAREC: (GHOST)
And yet you choose to ignore me, my Padawan.

VENTRESS:
I'm not your anything!

VENTRESS: (NARRATION)
I whirl around, expecting to see his face. Those crinkled eyes. That crooked smile.

But the room is empty, dust motes whirling in the moonlight.

He's not here. And yet . . .

KY NAREC: (GHOST)
How did you become this?

VENTRESS:
A monster?

KY NAREC:
(DISTORTED) Do not twist my words, little one.

VENTRESS:
Don't call me that.

KY NAREC:
(DISTORTED) What do you want me to call you?

VENTRESS:
You could try my name.

KY NAREC: (GHOST)
How did you become this, Asajj?

VENTRESS:
Actually, that's worse.

VENTRESS: (NARRATION)
I know I'm being contrary, but what does he expect? How did I come here? How did I become this woman? This creature?

He did this. He led me here.

He left me behind.

KY NAREC: (GHOST)
I never left you, Ventress. I never would.

VENTRESS:
Shut up! Get out of my head!

LEP-10019:
Mistress?

VENTRESS: (NARRATION)
The damn droid makes me jump. The castle is full of them, with their whirring servos and lifeless eyes.

VENTRESS:
I wasn't talking to you.

The droid looks around, its neck servos whirring.

LEP-10019:
There is no one else here.

VENTRESS:
No. No, there's not. (SIGHS) What do you want, droid?

LEP-10019:
My designation is LEP-10019.

VENTRESS:
I don't care.

LEP-10019:
Oh. Um. He needs you.

KY NAREC: (GHOST)
Ventress . . . please . . .

VENTRESS:
Lead the way.

SCENE 2. INT. CASTLE CORRIDOR.

The LEP-10019 droid clanks as it leads Ventress through the castle.

VENTRESS: (NARRATION)
I think of the ways I could destroy the waddling robot as it leads me through the castle. The corridors are long and as sterile as its workforce. As a building it's impressive, with its high vaulted ceilings and arched doors. We had nothing like it on Rattatak, nothing that wasn't pockmarked by laser burns anyway. But where are the portraits of long-dead ancestors? Where are the statues? Where is the stuffed rancor head mounted over a roaring hearth?

The castle is pristine but empty, devoid of warmth.

Like its master.

LEP-10019:
This way please.

VENTRESS: (NARRATION)
Dooku is in the great hall, standing on a raised dais. He stares through the circular window that dominates the far wall, his family's sigil etched into the stained glass.

LEP-10019:
Wait here.

VENTRESS: (NARRATION)
I fight the urge to separate the El-ee-pee's stupid rabbit-eared head from its narrow shoulders. It totters off, leaving me in Dooku's presence. The imposing man doesn't turn. He doesn't even acknowledge that I am here.

I wait, every muscle aching with the effort of appearing nonchalant.

As if I can fool him.

DOOKU:
Your feelings betray you.

VENTRESS:
I'm sorry. I—

DOOKU:
(STERN) Did I grant you permission to speak?

VENTRESS: (NARRATION)
I grit my teeth, trying to calm the fury that twists in my belly like a nest of bloodvipers.

DOOKU:
No. Let your anger grow. Let it seethe.

VENTRESS: (NARRATION)
Finally he turns, regarding me not with interest but with idle curiosity, the way a scientist examines a rodent to see if it has mastered a new trick, to see if it deserves a reward.

But there are no rewards here.

DOOKU:
Your burns are healing. Do they hurt?

VENTRESS:
No, Master.

DOOKU:
Liar. Try again.

VENTRESS:
Yes. They hurt very much.

DOOKU:
Good. Focus on the pain. Use it. It is the source of your power.

VENTRESS:
Yes, Master.

VENTRESS: (NARRATION)
Master. The word sticks in my throat. I vowed I would never call anyone Master again. Not after Hal'Sted. And especially not after Narec.

And yet, here I am.

KY NAREC: (GHOST)
Here you are.

VENTRESS: (NARRATION)
I clench my fists, nails biting into my palms. The voice has plagued me ever since I was brought here. A voice only I can hear. Unless this is another test? Has Dooku summoned a phantom to torment me?

I square my shoulders, raising my chin. I must appear strong.

Dooku's dark eyes narrow.

DOOKU:
You are troubled.

VENTRESS:
No, Master. It . . . It is nothing.

DOOKU:
I told you. Do not lie to me.

VENTRESS:
I wouldn't. I . . . I couldn't.

VENTRESS: (NARRATION)
A smile tugs at the corners of his mouth. The rat has performed well. Squeak, squeak, squeak.

DOOKU:
You wish to kill me.

VENTRESS:
No. I—

Force lightning crackles out from Dooku's fingers, striking Ventress.

VENTRESS:
(CRIES OUT)

VENTRESS: (NARRATION)
Dark lightning bursts from Dooku's fingers, coursing over me. In one agonizing, mind-shredding moment, he proves to me that nothing else matters. Not the droids. Not the castle. Not even Ky.

There is only his authority and his voice.

The lightning continues to flow throughout the scene as Dooku taunts her.

DOOKU:
Of course you want to kill me. You are a killer. That is what you do. That is why I chose you. Do you think I came to Rattatak by chance? That I somehow stumbled upon your pit?

VENTRESS:
(PAINED) No . . .

DOOKU:
The Force showed me. It showed me a Dathomiri sold to save her coven. A slave liberated from captivity. A Padawan forced to watch her Master bleed out in the dirt.

VENTRESS:
Please . . .

DOOKU:
Is that how they begged, your victims, as you took revenge, as you slaughtered every Rattataki who conspired to murder your Master? I wish I'd seen it, Ventress. I wish I'd seen their faces when they realized the storm they'd unleashed.

VENTRESS: (NARRATION)

Somehow, despite the lightning, despite the pain, I relive each and every moment. Feeling the fury swell inside me, my lightsabers a blur, their screams like music.

I never knew how sweet revenge would taste, how the fear in their eyes sated the anger in my belly.

Ky would have told me that it wasn't the Jedi way, but I didn't care. I had taken the Jedi way and rammed it down their throats along with my fist.

Zol Kramer. Rynn'k-lee. They all fell, one after another.

Until I faced Kirske. Until I faced the scumsnake who had ordered Ky's death.

I'd thought he'd be like the others. I thought he would pay. I thought he would suffer as I was suffering.

I was wrong. I was blindsided by my own vanity, so sure that I would emerge victorious. So convinced. I never expected Kirske to use himself as bait until it was too late, until I'd raced toward him, lightsabers blazing.

Until the trap had been sprung.

That's why Dooku found me, not surrounded by the corpses of my enemies, but forced to spill blood for the entertainment of others, a gladiator in a filthy pit, stun collar tight around my neck.

Could he sense my regret? My rage?

For my part, I had no idea who he was, just the latest in a long line of spectators enjoying the hospitality of Osika Kirske's viewing gallery. I had no idea he'd told Kirske he was looking for an assassin, or that he'd already made his choice.

I don't know who was more surprised when Dooku took Kirske's head, me or the Vollick himself. One minute Dooku was sipping wine from a crystal glass, and the next his crimson lightsaber was slicing through Kirske's neck.

The Vollick's head bounced down into the arena, a shocked expression on his face as it bounced once and then twice before coming to rest at my feet.

I couldn't celebrate. I couldn't revel in Kirske's death. I should've been the one to deal the killing blow, to snuff out his life, and yet this . . . this stranger with fine clothes and an imperious gaze had stolen my revenge.

I leapt from the arena floor, the Force propelling me up to the gallery, my lightsabers already burning. Dooku was waiting for me. Two blades against one. There was no way the old man should've been able to defend himself, and yet he did. He blocked every attack, parried every blow, giving no ground, taking no damage.

He didn't even spill his wine.

And then it came. His lightning. It felt like every atom in my body was being torn apart, every memory I had shredding beneath the onslaught. Mother Talzin. Hal'Sted. Ky. They were all gone, consumed in the pain of Dooku's dark magic.

I don't remember my lightsabers slipping from my hands. I don't even remember blacking out.

The next thing I knew, I was being grabbed by mechanical hands, dragged through unfamiliar corridors. My stun collar was gone, the air cool against my charred skin. I remember hearing birds as I was hauled past open windows. That's when I knew I was no longer on Rattatak. The only birds on Rattatak are the strike-vultures that strip bones clean on the dust plains.

He was waiting for me in the great hall, in the exact same place as he stands now, looking down at me with eyes as black as a starless sky.

"I will teach you the ways of the dark side, but first, you must prove yourself."

(A BEAT AS WE RETURN TO THE HERE AND NOW)

It takes me a moment to register that the lightning has stopped. Hands take my scorched arms. For a moment, I imagine it's Ky, helping me back to my feet, but then my vision clears and I'm looking into the face of my savior and tormentor.

I force myself to stand, telling myself I need to appear strong no matter what lessons Dooku inflicts.

DOOKU:
I don't want to have to do that again.

VENTRESS: (NARRATION)
That makes two of us.

He walks behind his desk, opening a drawer. As I struggle to draw air into my scorched lungs, he retrieves a disk no larger than a coin and tosses it toward me. It clatters and spins before coming to rest on the polished wood. I wait, not daring to move until he nods. Cautiously, I retrieve the disk, turning it over in my hand.

VENTRESS:
A data card?

DOOKU:
Place it in the holoprojector.

VENTRESS: (NARRATION)
I do as I am instructed, a hologram fizzing into existence. It's a boy, no older than ten years old, wearing the robes of a Jedi Initiate, hair buzz-cut short. There's something about his face. Something familiar.

VENTRESS:
(REALIZATION DAWNING) It's you.

DOOKU:
I'd forgotten I was ever that young. It belongs to my sister.

VENTRESS:
Your sister?

DOOKU:
I had no idea she kept the recordings. I told her to destroy them. She disobeyed me.

VENTRESS:
But I don't understand. You were a Jedi.

DOOKU:
I was.

VENTRESS:
But I thought Jedi cut all ties to their family.

DOOKU:
They do. But my sister . . . let's just say . . . we found each other . . .

VENTRESS:
How?

VENTRESS: (NARRATION)
I tense, waiting for another burst of lightning, but instead Dooku's eyes drop away, focusing on the hologram of the boy in front of us. I sense conflict in him, memories long buried bubbling to the surface. When he speaks again, there is a . . . wistfulness in his voice, a vulnerability that I just haven't heard in him before.

DOOKU:
I never knew my family, for the reasons you mentioned. Like most of the Order, I was brought to the Temple by a Seeker, a Jedi who was tasked to scour the galaxy for Force-sensitive infants. I had no recollection of my home, having been transported to Coruscant as a babe in arms, only to be told that I was to return as an Initiate.

VENTRESS:
Return to Serenno. Why?

DOOKU:
For a great celebration . . .

A long time ago in a galaxy far, far away. . . .

Join up! Subscribe to our newsletter
at ReadStarWars.com or find us on social.

 StarWarsBooks

 @DelReyStarWars

 @DelReyStarWars